ICE I

Most of the fourteen men began firing even before they were within effective range.

"Clint?" Annie said, her voice quavering.

"Not yet," Cody said, sighting down the barrel of his own rifle. "Wait for Clint."

Clint looked over at the others. They had each pulled over a barrel or knocked over a bench or a bale of hay to use for cover. Delvecchio and Cody looked calm; Annie looked frazzled, and Frank Butler wiped the sweat from his eyes with his sleeve. Clint knew he could count on Cody, felt he could on Delvecchio, but if Annie and Butler faltered, they were going to be in trouble.

The men were still shooting, and now their lead was striking the ground or whizzing by. Still, Clint did not give the order to fire.

"Clint . . . ," Butler said.

And still they came.

"Clint . . . ," Delvecchio said.

"Closer . . . ," Clint said.

"By God, man," Buffalo Bill Cody said, "you are going to use that gun, aren't you?"

THE GUNSMITH

LITTLE SURESHOT AND THE WILD WEST SHOW

J. R. ROBERTS

J

JOVE BOOKS, NEW YORK

THE BERKLEY PUBLISHING GROUP
Published by the Penguin Group
Penguin Group (USA) Inc.
375 Hudson Street, New York, New York 10014, USA
Penguin Group (Canada), 10 Alcorn Avenue, Toronto, Ontario M4V 3B2, Canada
(a division of Pearson Penguin Canada Inc.)
Penguin Books Ltd., 80 Strand, London WC2R 0RL, England
Penguin Group Ireland, 25 St. Stephen's Green, Dublin 2, Ireland (a division of Penguin Books Ltd.)
Penguin Group (Australia), 250 Camberwell Road, Camberwell, Victoria 3124, Australia
(a division of Pearson Australia Group Pty. Ltd.)
Penguin Books India Pvt. Ltd., 11 Community Centre, Panchsheel Park, New Delhi—110 017, India
Penguin Group (NZ), Cnr. Airborne and Rosedale Roads, Albany, Auckland 1310, New Zealand
(a division of Pearson New Zealand Ltd.)
Penguin Books (South Africa) (Pty.) Ltd., 24 Sturdee Avenue, Rosebank, Johannesburg 2196, South
Africa

Penguin Books Ltd., Registered Offices: 80 Strand, London WC2R 0RL, England

This is a work of fiction. Names, characters, places, and incidents either are the product of the author's imagination or are used fictitiously, and any resemblance to actual persons, living or dead, business establishments, events, or locales is entirely coincidental.

LITTLE SURESHOT AND THE WILD WEST SHOW

A Jove Book / published by arrangement with the author

PRINTING HISTORY
Jove edition / November 2004

ISBN: 0-515-13851-7

JOVE®
Jove is an imprint of The Berkley Publishing Group,
a division of Penguin Group (USA) Inc.
375 Hudson Street, New York, New York 10014.
JOVE and the "J" design are trademarks belonging to Penguin Group (USA) Inc.

PRINTED IN THE UNITED STATES OF AMERICA

10 9 8 7 6 5 4 3 2 1

PROLOGUE

Clint did not even know Capt. Jason Handy that well, but the man was a legendary figure in the Texas Rangers and he felt it incumbent upon him to pay his last respects. Add to that the fact that he had already planned to leave Labyrinth and head north, anyway, and this pretty much made Fort Worth just a stop along the way.

The wake was being held in a saloon, which was apparently fitting, since Handy not only had a reputation as a tough Ranger, but a hard drinker, as well. He was actually a retired Ranger when he died—since there weren't too many seventy-seven-year-olds still serving—and it was a group of his old unit who had pooled their money to give him a great wake and funeral.

Clint was returning from the final night of the wake, walking through the lobby of the Emporia Hotel, when the desk clerk caught his eye and waved him over.

"This arrived for you just a little while ago, sir," the man said, handing him a telegram.

"Thank you."

"Another arrived for you this afternoon, shortly after you left, and we slipped that one underneath your door."

"Well," Clint said, "thanks again."

He carried the second telegram to his room and picked the first one up off the floor when he entered, wondering who even knew he was here except for Rick Hartman in Labyrinth.

As it turned out both were forwarded by Rick, and both had originated in New York City.

The first was from Buffalo Bill Cody, who had just returned to New York after touring with his Wild West Show in Europe. He was going to be spending a little less than a year in New York—specifically in Staten Island— and he was inviting Clint to come to New York—all expenses paid—to discuss the possibility of working with the show during that time. Cody had tried to get Clint to join his show before, but Clint had always refused. He probably would have refused this time, too, except he hadn't been to New York in some time, not since he'd met P. T. Barnum there and received his Darley Arabian, Eclipse, as a gift from the great showman.

Cody, himself, was also a great showman—and a friend—and an all-expenses-paid trip to New York was hard to resist.

However, it was more the second telegram that convinced him than the first. That one came from Frank Butler. Butler was an old friend, a professional sharpshooter who had worked for Cody for a long time. He was also married to Cody's famed female sharpshooter Annie Oakley. He'd married Annie back in '76, when she was all of sixteen, and although Clint had seen Butler a time or two since then, he had never met Annie.

But even more convincing than the opportunity for an all-expenses-paid trip and a chance to meet the famous "Little Sureshot" was the tone of the telegram. Butler was asking Clint to come to New York to help him.

Specifically, the last line of the missive said, "Annie and I could really use your help."

Clint folded both telegrams and set them down on top of the chest of drawers. He walked to the window, folded his arms and stared down at the street. Apparently, both Frank and Annie had a problem that they could not solve between them. He wondered if Cody knew about Butler's telegram, and vice versa. If not, then it was a coincidence that they had both sent him one at the same time, and he hated coincidences. He was a firm believer that no good ever came of them.

Still, a friend was asking for help, and when in his life was he ever able to resist that?

He had the funeral in the morning, and then he could go to the railroad station with Eclipse and get a ticket east. Luckily, he had no firm plans after the burial tomorrow, and he was able to head off for New York at a moment's notice. It was what he truly liked about his life, the ability to make a decision like this quickly, and without consulting anyone else.

Further proof—not that he needed it—that Clint Adams would have made a terrible bank teller, or husband.

ONE

Clint took a cab from the train station directly to the Waldorf, the same hotel he had stayed in the last time he was there. After he signed the register, the clerk read the name and then smiled broadly. He was trained to recognize celebrities.

"Ah, Mr. Adams, sir," he said, "so nice to have you back with us. A room overlooking the street?"

"Thank you, yes, that would be fine."

"Will you need help with your luggage?"

"No, thank you," he said, looking down at his suitcase. "I have just one."

"And do you have a horse that needs care?"

"No." Clint had decided to leave Eclipse behind in Fort Worth, in the care of his friend Luke Short, who owned and operated the White Elephant Saloon.

"Very well," the clerk said, handing him his key. "Since you have been here before, I'll just give you the key and let you go to your room. Enjoy your stay, please."

"Thank you," Clint said. "I will."

He found his way to his room on the second floor, dropped his suitcase on the bed and then went to the window and slid the heavy brocade curtain open so he could look down at Park Avenue. New York always excited Clint; it was so different from anywhere else in the country—or the world, for that matter. He'd been to Denver, and Chicago and Philadelphia, and as far as London, England, and nothing compared with New York City.

He moved away from the window and checked the time. Frank Butler knew he was arriving today, and they had made arrangements to have dinner together. He had two hours to change his clothes and meet Butler down in the lobby, which meant he had plenty of time to go out and buy a suit.

He only had to go down the street to find a store where he bought a black suit and a white shirt suitable to wear to dinner in the Waldorf's restaurant. He took them back to his room, and while he changed he wondered if Annie would be with Frank when they met for dinner.

Once he was finished dressing, he dug his little Colt New Line out of his suitcase, because wearing a gun belt on the streets of New York was frowned upon. He tucked the New Line into his belt at the small of his back and then left the room to meet Butler.

Frank Butler was waiting in the lobby when Clint came down. He was a tall, handsome, dark-haired man in his thirties, wearing a black suit much like the one Clint had put on. As Clint came down the stairs, Butler spotted him and, smiling, came across the floor to meet him.

"Clint," he said, happily, "it's real good to see you."

"Frank." The two men shook hands vigorously.

"I'm sorry Annie couldn't come," Butler said. "She had, uh, something else to do tonight."

"Hey, that's fine," Clint said. "We'll get to catch up. We're eating here, right?"

"It's a good a place as any, in New York," Butler said. "Annie and I have our favorites, but we'll show them to you another time."

They talked and caught up a bit while they walked through the lobby to the restaurant and waited to be seated. Clint told Butler about the funeral he had just come from and named some of the famous lawmen he had run into there. Butler was suitably impressed, but Clint could see that something was bothering the man, even while he was listening.

Once they were seated, they both ordered steaks and beer and then Clint waited for Butler to get to the point, which he did fairly quickly.

"Clint," Butler said, "I know I didn't tell you much in that telegram."

"You told me you needed help, Frank," Clint said. "That was enough to get me here."

"Well . . . I'd like to explain why I asked you to come."

"And I'd like to hear it."

"You haven't met Annie yet," Butler said, "so all you know about her is what you've heard."

"That she's a crack shot."

"The best shot I ever saw," Butler said. "When she beat me back in '76—a mere girl of sixteen—I was stunned, and she's only gotten better. Why, I bet she could even beat . . . well, you."

"Go on." Clint was wondering if the comment was innocent, or dangled as some kind of bait.

"Well, she is a great shot—and so am I, by the way— but I have to tell you the truth, neither of us has ever had to fire our guns at . . . at a live target."

"You've fired at pigeons. I know you have." Clint knew that some of the contests Annie and Frank Butler had competed in over the years had involved live birds.

"I don't mean animals," Butler said. "I mean . . . people."

"Ah," Clint said, "you mean neither of you has ever been involved in a gun battle of any kind."

"Right," Butler said. "We're performers, not gun . . . people." "Gun*men*" would not have applied to them both.

"What's your point here, Frank?"

Butler took a deep breath, then said, "Annie's been gettin' some threats on her life, Clint. And we don't know what to do about it."

TWO

"What do you mean 'threats'?" Clint asked. "How?"

"Well, first I should tell you we're not with Cody anymore."

"What? When did that happen?"

"Earlier this year," Butler said. "We left him in Europe and came back."

"What have you been doing?"

"We were with another show, but it was real low class, you know? So we came to New York and we've been freelancing."

"Well, okay," Clint said, "it's up to the two of you what you want to do for a living. What's this got to do with being threatened?"

"There's this man who has come to a couple of our

shows, and he seems to have become . . . obsessed with Annie."

"Obsessed? You mean, he's in love with her?"

"We don't know for sure," Butler said. "He's been at some of our shows, and then suddenly we began to see him on the street. Annie saw him following her a few times."

"Has he ever done more than follow her?" Clint asked. "Has he approached her? Talked to her? Touched her?"

"No. She said all he does is follow her."

"What about when you're together?"

"I haven't seen him," Butler said, with a shrug. "I guess he spots me and then doesn't show himself."

"Have you ever tried following her yourself, to see if he follows her?" Clint asked.

"A couple of times," Butler said. "If he was there, he didn't show himself."

The waiter arrived with their dinners, and also placed their beers next to their plates.

"Anything else, gentlemen?"

"Not just now," Clint said, "and if you don't mind, we'll be having a conversation for the rest of the evening, so don't come to the table unless we signal to you." To soften the blow of his words, Clint gave the man an early tip.

"As you wish, sir," the waiter said, not insulted at all.

Each of them picked up his knife and fork and attacked the perfectly prepared steaks, but they continued their conversation.

"Frank, is that why Annie's not here tonight?" Clint asked. "She was afraid he would follow you?"

"No," Butler said. "Annie's meeting with Cody. Apparently he wants us back."

"I have a meeting with him tomorrow," Clint said. "He sent me a telegram the same time you did."

Butler paused and almost put down his fork, but recovered his composure admirably.

"Well," he said, "maybe he only wants her back, then. That would be quite an attraction, 'Annie Oakley versus The Gunsmith.' "

"I'd never sign up if it was to replace you."

"You wouldn't be replacing me," Butler said, "because I'm not even with the show now."

"Well, it doesn't matter," Clint said. "He's invited me to join the show before."

"See what his offer is," Butler suggested.

"I intend to," Clint said, "but let's get back to your problem. What exactly do you want me to do?"

This time Butler did lay down his fork.

"We want you to find him and make him go away," he said.

"Frank . . . why can't you do that yourself?"

"There's something I didn't tell you."

"What's that?"

"He's a gunman," Butler said. "He competed against us in a contest some time ago."

"How did he do?"

"He lost."

"Then what do you have to fear?"

"He's not as good a shot as we are," Butler said, "but he's faster, and he's killed before. We haven't."

"So you think that if you threaten him he won't believe you."

"Not at all."

"And you won't kill him, and he knows that."

Butler looked away. "Yes."

"Frank . . . if Annie's life depended on it, you'd kill him."

"Yes," Butler said, looking at Clint, "I think I would—or I'd try. But I don't think I could take him, Clint. Not face to face, gun to gun. That's not what I do."

"No," Clint said, "it's what I do."

"I didn't mean—I'm not trying to hire your gun—"

"I know that," Clint said. "Come on, finish your steak. You know I'll do what I can to help you."

"Thank you," Butler said, picking up his knife and fork. "Annie and I will be very grateful."

"Tomorrow I have a dinner with Cody," Clint said. "Why don't you and I and Annie have lunch?"

"He never shows himself when I'm with her," Butler said. "What makes you think he'll show himself when the two of us are with her?"

"Maybe he won't," Clint said. "Maybe he'll see that there are two of us now and he'll decide to leave her alone."

"Maybe," Butler added, hopefully, "he'll recognize you and go away."

"Maybe," Clint said, "but I was really just thinking of meeting Annie and getting her to trust me."

"She'll trust you," Butler said. "Take my word for it."

"Still," Clint said, "the first step will be meeting each other."

"All right," Butler said, "that's what we'll do, then."

After dinner they each had a cup of coffee and a piece of pie.

"You know," Butler said, "Cody would pay you a lot to team up with Annie."

"And he'd pay her a lot, too."

"I suppose."

"Are you telling me you want me to take the job?"

"If I swallow my pride," Butler said, "I'll admit that it would be good for all of us."

"Not for me," Clint said. "I don't really want to be part of a Wild West show."

"It's not a bad life."

"I'm sure it's not," Clint said. "It's just not for me, Frank."

"Well," Butler said, "I guess it's not for everyone."

After dessert they went back out to the lobby and parted company there. Butler was going to go back to the hotel where he was living with Annie and find out how her meeting with Cody went.

Clint walked his friend to the front door, shook hands and then watched him walk down Park Avenue, checking to see if anyone was following him. Either no one was— or Clint just couldn't see him.

THREE

Vernon Weeks had a choice that evening. He could follow Annie Oakley or her husband, Frank Butler. Since he knew Annie was going to have dinner with Buffalo Bill Cody, he decided to follow Butler and see who he was having dinner with.

After Butler entered the Waldorf lobby, Weeks crossed the street so he could look inside. He saw Butler meet a man as he came down the stairs. A guest in the hotel, obviously. They went into the restaurant and Weeks entered the hotel.

By the time he left the hotel an hour later, he knew who Butler had been meeting, and he was excited by it. He crossed the street to wait for Butler to leave. He had to wait two hours, but he was a very patient man. He watched as Butler left, and he saw that Clint Adams was

watching Butler walk away. Adams also looked up and
down the street, obviously checking to see if anyone else
was watching or following Butler. Weeks was well
enough hidden, so Adams eventually turned around and
went back inside the hotel. Weeks doubted that a man like
Clint Adams was going to turn in this early, so once again
he quit his hiding place, crossed the street and entered the
hotel.

Clint went back into the Waldorf, walked across the side
of the lobby opposite the restaurant and entered the bar.
He went over to the bartender and said, "Beer, please."

"Comin' up, sir," the barman said. "Are you a guest?"

"Yes," Clint said, and gave the man his room number.

"Very good, sir."

Clint picked up his beer and turned around to survey
the room. All of the men seated at the tables were dressed
in suits like his, in varying colors—browns, blues, grays
and some black. He was sure they were either guests or
businessmen who liked to drink in the Waldorf bar after
work. He couldn't blame them. The bar was plush, smelling of expensive leather, all deep browns and reds, with
ornate crystal light fixtures, and oil paintings on every
wall. It was a place for men to drink, and—at the moment,
anyway—there were no women there.

He finished his beer and set the mug back down on the
bar.

"Another?" the bartender asked.

"No, that's fine."

"Charge it to your room?"

"Please."

Clint left the bar and entered the lobby again. Briefly
he considered going to his room, but he wasn't quite that

tired yet, even with the amount of time he'd spent traveling.

He decided to go for a walk.

Weeks watched Clint Adams have a beer in the bar and speak to no one but the bartender. He didn't seem interested in doing anything but drinking his beer. After he finished, he turned and came back toward the lobby. Weeks retreated behind a large potted plant and watched as Adams paused in the lobby then headed for the door. He went through it, out onto Park Avenue.

Weeks crossed the lobby and went out the door after Adams. He watched as the man known as The Gunsmith turned and started walking north.

Weeks stepped out into the street with the intention of following, but then decided against it. A man like The Gunsmith would not easily be followed. Weeks had found out what he wanted to know, anyway. Frank Butler had called The Gunsmith for help. Now what Vernon Weeks had to do was call somebody equally as dangerous to help him, maybe even things up a bit.

But then again, Oakley and Butler were entertainers. They fired their guns in fun. Weeks doubted they had ever fired them in anger. So maybe he didn't need a lot of help. Maybe he needed just a little.

Clint simply walked around the block in order to check and see if he was being followed. He didn't spot anyone, so either they were very good, or there was no one there. When he got back to the front door of the hotel, he went inside and returned to his room for the night.

Suddenly, he was very tired.

FOUR

In the morning Clint took a leisurely bath in his room—one of the luxuries he really enjoyed about the Waldorf—then dressed and had an equally leisurely breakfast in the Waldorf's restaurant. After that, he decided to go out and walk around New York in the daylight, maybe up to Central Park. Before he got involved in whatever trouble Frank Butler and his wife were in, he wanted just a few hours to enjoy this city he liked so much.

Frank Butler came back from his own bath and found his wife, the famous Annie Oakley, staring out the hotel window.

"Honey," he said, "it's all going to be okay now that Clint is here."

"I can't help it," she said, turning to face him. "I can

19

feel him out there. If Cody hadn't come directly here and picked me up last night, he would have followed me, I know it."

Butler walked over to his wife and wrapped his arms around her. She was a little thing, but she was a strong woman—usually. This business with this man who was apparently stalking her was getting to her.

Last night she had told Butler about her meeting with Cody . . .

Buffalo Bill had offered her a lot of money to come back to the show, even if it was only for the time they would be playing out on Staten Island. She had told Cody she wouldn't work without her husband. Cody asked her to think it over. Teaming with The Gunsmith, he told her, would be good for everyone.

"You don't have The Gunsmith signed, Colonel."

"Ah, but I will, after he hears my offer at dinner tomorrow night," Cody replied.

"Well," she said, "if and when you get him, maybe we'll talk about it again."

At that point in her story last night her husband said, "You didn't just tell him no?"

"Frank," she'd said, "he's offering a lot—and I mean a lot—of money, and we're just about broke. Where's the harm working just while he's on Staten Island?"

"With The Gunsmith."

"Well, that's what he's offering all the money for," she said. "The teaming of Adams and me."

"Annie—"

"Can we sleep on it and talk about it in the mornin'?" she'd asked.

And that's what they had done . . .

• • •

Now he held his wife tightly in his arms and felt her shaking, and he couldn't bear to bring it up, even though it bothered him that she hadn't just told Cody straight out, "No, not without my husband."

Once again—as he had done last night with Clint Adams—he thought that if he set aside his male pride, this was a very good deal for them. Of course, if Clint didn't go for it, it would be another story.

"Let's go and get some breakfast," he said finally, patting her shoulder and letting her go.

"Not a big one," she said. "We have lunch with your friend, and I don't want to be full for that."

"All right."

"I'm excited to meet him," she said. "He's a legend like Cody."

"You're a legend, my Little Sureshot, or have you forgotten?" Butler asked.

"I'm not a legend," she said, "not compared to them. They are truly giants of their time."

"Well," Butler said, "I'm sure when you meet Clint, you'll see he's just a man—and a good friend."

"Whatever else he is," she said, "he's a legend. There's no denying that."

Just for a moment, while his wife dressed, Butler couldn't help but feel a bit jealous of Clint Adams.

Outside the hotel of Mr. and Mrs. Butler, Vernon Weeks stood across the street, watching their window. He saw Annie standing there, and then Butler come over and take her in his arms. He wasn't the sharpshooter each of them was, but he felt sure he could pick Butler off right from there, if he wanted to.

He just didn't want to.

Weeks was still out there when Annie and Butler left their hotel to walk to a nearby café for breakfast. He knew where they usually ate, so there was really no reason to follow them. He just wanted to start off the day with a glimpse of Annie Oakley. He could feel her fear, almost smell it on the air, and he needed that to keep him going.

Now he turned and walked the opposite way, for as much as he hated the newfangled instrument, he had some important telephone calls to make.

FIVE

Clint had agreed to meet Frank and Annie at a hotel nearby, on Third Avenue. It was one of those favorite places Butler had talked about the night before.

He got there early so he'd be able to watch them as they approached. They made an odd couple, the tall, dark man and the slight, light-haired gal next to him. From where Clint stood Annie Oakley could still have been the sixteen-year-old girl Frank Butler married over a dozen years before.

As they crossed the street and approached him in front of the restaurant, he could see no one following them, or even paying them any special attention. And yet he had the feeling someone was there, just as he'd had the feeling last night that someone was watching his room. He'd stopped to look out the window before turning in, and it was then he got the feeling he was being watched. He wondered if whoever this man was, he already knew that Frank Butler had asked for help. What would his reaction be to that? Clint wondered.

Would it deter him?

Or challenge him?

Only time would tell.

Annie was smiling broadly as they reached him, and she was the first to speak.

"Clint Adams," she said. "I'm so thrilled to meet you at last."

"Annie Oakley," Clint said, "the pleasure is all mine."

The two shook hands rather awkwardly on the street, unsure of whether or not they should do anything else.

"Why don't we go inside?" Butler suggested.

"Ladies first," Clint said, and held the door open for Annie. Butler gave him a meaningful look—he had seen Clint checking behind them—and Clint shook his head, no.

They went inside and found a table, and were served by a man who knew Annie and Butler personally. He was fiftyish, squat and bald, but very well manicured and clean. Clint could smell some kind of soap coming off the man.

"How nice to have you here again so soon," he said, "and you've brought a friend."

"Gunther, this is our friend, and a legend of the Old West, Clint Adams," Annie said, but Butler nudged her before she could add, "The Gunsmith."

"Well, I'm very happy to have you in my restaurant," Gunther said. "Perhaps a bottle of wine, on the house?"

"It's a little early for wine, Gunther," Annie said, answering for all of them—which suited Clint. He didn't want wine, but also didn't want to insult the owner of the restaurant. "How about a pot of your wonderful coffee?"

"Excellent choice," Gunther said. "I will leave you to look at the menus and take care of that right away."

"I didn't notice the name of the restaurant when I came in," Clint said to the Butlers.

"There's no name on the outside," Annie said, "but everyone calls it 'Gunther's.' The coffee is excellent, and I remember Frank saying you liked good coffee."

Actually, Clint liked "strong" coffee—the stronger the better, like trail coffee—but he said, "I'm looking forward to it. What should I order?"

"They have a great beef stew," Annie said.

"Sold." Clint put the menu down and did not look at it again.

"Me, too," Butler said.

"All right," Annie said, "I'll make it three."

Clint had the distinct impression that Annie's bright mood was forced. He believed that she was glad to meet him, but everything else was coming off insincere.

Gunther returned with the pot of coffee and three cups and took their orders for three beef stews. Clint could tell the coffee would be good before he tasted it, because it was pitch black, and he could smell how strong it was.

"Annie," he said, "I wonder if we could talk about the problem you and Frank are having? And forget about trying to be cheerful?"

Annie stared at him for a moment, then her shoulders fell.

"Was I that obvious?" she asked.

"Just a little."

"I don't mind telling you, Clint, I'm scared."

"Do you think this man wants to hurt you?"

"I think he might hurt Frank" she said honestly. "I'm not worried about myself."

"Well, I'm worried about you," Frank said, putting his arm around her.

"Let's worry about both of you for a while, shall we?" Clint asked. "Did you see this man last night when you had dinner with Cody?"

"No."

"This morning?"

"No."

Clint decided not to tell the couple that he had had the feeling he was being watched, already. They had enough to worry about.

"Okay, why don't you give me a description of him, for a start?"

They both started talking at once, and then Butler stopped and deferred to his wife. She described the man as in his late thirties, tall, rangy, usually with several days' growth of stubble which was not quite a beard. He wore dark clothes, including a black jacket, which she was sure was hiding a gun in a shoulder rig.

"He looks like a gambler, to tell you the truth," she finished.

"So this is not some young man who is sweet on you," Clint said.

"Not at all," she said.

"When was the first time you saw him?"

"We competed in a contest in New Jersey," Annie said. "Well, actually, I did. It involved shooting at live pigeons. It came down to him and me, and I won. He was very good, though, and he came over to congratulate me. He . . . he kissed my hand when he did."

"That doesn't sound threatening."

"It was . . . creepy," she said, "and I'm not sure why."

"Okay, when did you see him again?"

"Another contest," she said, "also in New Jersey. It involved shooting clay pigeons from a mechanized trap. Again, he was very good, but I won and he came in second. Once again he came over to congratulate."

"Did he kiss your hand?"

"I didn't give him the chance," she said. "I think it made him angry when I pulled my hand away."

"Did you see him at any more competitions after that?"

"Yes," she said, "quite a few, but as a spectator, not a competitor. He just came and . . . watched me."

"It was soon after that," Frank Butler said, "that she saw him on the street."

"What was he doing?" Clint asked.

"Just standing across the street . . . watching," she said. "I was alone, and when I started to walk, he fell in behind me and just . . . followed me. He was there the entire day!"

"She came home rattled and told me what happened," Butler said. "I went outside immediately, but he wasn't there."

"After that," she said, "he followed me two more times when I went out alone. I . . . I couldn't go out, anymore. Not without Frank along."

"Did you ever see him on the street?" Clint asked Frank.

"Once," Butler said.

"What happened?"

Butler paused. "I'm not proud of this."

Annie placed her hand on her husband's arm.

"You have nothing to be ashamed of, Frank."

Before Butler could reply, Gunther interrupted them and served three bowls of hot beef stew.

"Please enjoy," he said, and withdrew, with Annie thanking him and gracing him with a smile. Clint could see that the man was completely smitten with her. At least he wasn't following her around, though.

"Frank?" he said, wanting the man to continue with his story.

"Taste the beef stew first," Butler said, "and then I'll tell you what happened."

SIX

"We came out one morning, after he had followed her three times, and there he was, standing across the street," Butler explained while they ate. "I told Annie to wait, and I went across to talk to him . . ."

The man was leaning against a lamppost as Frank Butler crossed the street toward him, and as Butler got closer the man smiled at him, but didn't speak.

"What do you think you're doing?" Butler demanded when he reached him.

The man shrugged, looking unconcerned, and said, "I'm just standin' on the corner, Mr. Butler. Is there a law against that?"

"You know who I am."

"Course I do," the man said, then nodded at Annie,

standing across the street, and said, "I know who your lovely wife is, too."

"Look," Butler said, "you can't keep doing this."

"Doin' what?" the man asked, shrugging again. "I'm just standin' on the corner."

"You've been following my wife," Butler said. "You've done it for three days now."

"So?"

Butler was taken aback for a moment.

"You're not going to deny it?"

"What if I have been followin' her?" the man asked. "What are you gonna do about it?"

"I'm—Well, I'm . . . I'll go to the police."

"The police," the man said, shaking his head. "The great Frank Butler, crack shot that you are, married to Annie Oakley, and you're gonna go to the police?" The man pushed himself off the pole and stood up straight. "Why don't you make me stop, Mr. Butler?" he asked. "You got a gun on you?"

"Of course not," Butler said. "I don't walk around in New York with a gun on me."

"Well now, that's a damn shame," the man said. "See, 'cause I got a gun on me, and if you had one, we could settle this right here and now, like two men."

"This is not Dodge City," Butler said. "You can't—"

"You ever been to Dodge City?" the man asked, interrupting him.

"What? No, I haven't. What's that got to do—"

"Well, I have," the man said. "Fact is, I've killed men in Dodge City, and in other towns in the West." He stepped closer to Butler and poked him in the chest with his forefinger. "You see, I've shot at live men, Mr. Butler, while you have only shot at clay targets and glass balls and pigeons. You're an entertainer, and I'm a gunman."

"So what?" Butler asked, trying not to show how nervous he was. "I told you, this is not the Old West."

"But this is still the way men settle things, Mr. Butler," the man said.

"What have we to settle?" Butler asked.

"You want me to stop followin' your wife, right?"

"Of course."

"Then meet me," the man said, "meet me in the park with your gun strapped on, and we'll see who the better man is."

"That's crazy," Butler said. "Why would you want to do that?"

"To show her who the better man is."

"So you want to shoot targets with me to prove—"

"Don't be a fool!" the man said loudly. He backed up a step. "I'm talkin' about you, me and our guns, face to face. You know what I'm talkin' about."

"You *are* crazy," Butler said. "I'm going to call the police."

"Go ahead," the man said. "I won't be here when they get here."

"Good!" Butler said.

"But I'll be around, Butler," the man said, dropping the "mister." "I'll always be around."

Butler backed away from the man, then turned and went back across the street to where Annie was waiting . . .

"He was right," Butler said. "By the time we got the police there, he was gone. But they looked at me . . . funny."

"Funny how?" Clint asked.

"Like they wondered why I'd need them to fight my

battles for me. The way I look at myself in the mirror now."

"That's silly," Clint said. "As you've already told me, you're an entertainer, a showman, not a gunman. If he is a gunman, you'd be foolish to face him as he asked."

"That's what I told him," Annie said. "He thinks he should have faced him. He thinks that's what most men would have done."

"And most men would have died," Clint said. "You did the right thing, Frank."

"It doesn't feel like it."

"Nevertheless," Clint said, "you did." While listening to Butler's story, he had eaten his beef stew. Now he pushed the empty bowl away from him. "Do we know this man's name?"

"We checked with the people who ran one of the New Jersey contests," Annie said. "He entered as Vernon Weeks."

"Weeks?"

"Do you know him?" Butler asked.

Clint gave the name some thought. There was something familiar about it, but he couldn't place it.

"No," he said, "I don't know Vernon Weeks, but before this is all over, I will."

SEVEN

They left the restaurant after praising the food to a very happy Gunther. He asked them all to come back soon.

Outside they looked up and down the street but saw no one watching them.

"No one on the street seems interested in us," Annie said, "but he's out there. I can feel him."

"All right," Clint said. "You two go back to your hotel. Tomorrow morning, Annie, at nine A.M., you go for a walk."

"To where?"

"It doesn't matter," Clint said. "Just go for a walk. I'll be there, and if this Weeks is around I'll take care of him."

"You'll kill him?" Annie asked.

"Well," Clint said, "he hasn't done anything yet to warrant killing him, has he?"

"N-no . . ."

"So how about I just have a talk with him, first?"

"That makes sense," Butler said.

"Can you walk to your hotel from here?" Clint asked.

"No," Butler said, "we'll have to catch a cab or a trolley."

"Okay, I'll walk along with you until you catch one," Clint said. As they started walking, he asked, "Annie, how did your dinner with Buffalo Bill go?"

"He wants to team us up," she said. "You and me, Clint."

"I have a dinner with him tonight."

"He's going to throw a lot of money at you."

"Let him, Annie," Clint said. "If he wants you, he'll have to take Frank, too."

"You'll turn him down?" she asked. "No matter how much money he offers you?"

"I'm not a showman," Clint said. "It's as simple as that."

He walked with them for half a block before they were able to flag down a passing cabbie. Clint held the horse while they climbed on board, then waved as they pulled away. He stood there for a moment looking around, but there was still no sign of anyone watching him.

He was walking distance from the Waldorf, so he took a leisurely stroll back there, keeping especially alert for anyone following him. By the time he reached the Park Avenue entrance he had spotted no one.

As he entered the lobby, he hoped no one had, indeed, followed him, because if they had they were too good for him to spot. That was not a very comforting thought.

Unfortunately, he didn't pay much attention to the

lobby itself, which was filled with people—two of whom were paying him particular attention . . .

"See him?" Weeks asked.

"I see 'im."

"That's your man," Weeks said.

"The Gunsmith, himself?"

"That's him."

"He don't look like much," the other man said.

"Well, he is," Weeks said. "I mean, if any part of his reputation is for real."

"Can't believe everything you read in dime novels," the second man said.

Weeks stood up as Clint entered the bar.

"Well, he's yours, now," he said. "You can take the time to find out. I've got other things to do."

"Like what?"

Weeks gave the seated man a hard stare.

"My business," he said. "You just tend to yours and don't worry about me."

With that Weeks walked out of the Waldorf lobby.

EIGHT

That night, when he left to meet Cody for dinner, it became very clear to Clint that he was now being followed. Either the person had become careless, or it was somebody different.

Once again he had managed to arrange a meal that was walking distance from his hotel. It was during that walk that he spotted his tail. The man was laying back a couple of blocks, and walking across the street, but it was still obvious—especially since Clint had already seen him in the lobby.

He decided to go ahead and let the man follow him all he wanted for now. He was going to concentrate on his dinner with Buffalo Bill Cody, which was taking place in a Madison Avenue steak house called Morton's.

Cody was already there and seated when Clint arrived.

He waved when Clint entered, and stood up. A tall man in his late forties, Cody was as dramatic looking a figure as Clint had ever seen, with his well-cared-for beard and mustache and long, flowing hair. He had earned all the accolades that had ever been heaped upon him, as a buffalo hunter, a Pony Express rider and an Indian Scout, among other things. Now he was a consummate showman, along with P. T. Barnum, who Clint had discovered was in England at the moment.

"Clint Adams," Cody said. "By God, it's good to see you, boy."

They were close to each other in age, but Cody had a habit of treating all people as if they were younger than he was.

"Have a seat," he said, shaking hands vigorously. "I ordered some coffee, but maybe you'd like somethin' stronger?"

"I'll get a beer with dinner, Bill," Clint said, "but coffee's fine for now."

"How the hell are you, man?" Cody asked, pouring a cup for Clint. "It's been ages."

"A lot of years, Bill."

"Well, catch me up then," Cody said. He spread his arms. "My life's an open book, so you probably know I just got back from Europe."

"So I heard," Clint said. "Me, I've pretty much been staying in this country."

"Well," Cody said, "if that's a problem for you, I can change that, you know."

"You going to make me an offer even before we've ordered dinner, Bill?"

Cody laughed, attracting the attention of the people in the restaurant who weren't already gawking at him. He was in full buckskin regalia, and his booming voice carried across the entire restaurant.

"No, no," he said, "you go ahead and order, although if you order anything but a steak they'll probably toss you out of here."

"Steak it is, then." Clint put the menu down.

"Good," Cody said, "because I already ordered us two steak dinners, and here they come."

Clint turned and saw a white-coated waiter walking across the restaurant carrying a tray with two steak dinners on it. When he reached their table, he distributed the plates with a flourish. Clint saw that Cody had ordered every kind of trimming possible. There were vegetables of every size and color imaginable, and a basket of fresh rolls, to boot. Before the waiter left, Clint ordered a beer, and Cody asked for one, as well.

"Well," Clint said, "you're paying, so how could I complain?"

"You can't," Cody said. "I was counting on that. Dig in, lad, dig in. We'll talk business when we've finished eatin'—but you still have to catch me up."

So Clint told Cody about some of the things that had been happening to him. He included his last adventure in New York, when he met P. T. Barnum, as well as the funeral he had just come from in Fort Worth.

"P. T. Barnum!" Cody said. "What a showman he is, eh?"

"Amazing," Clint said, "as you are, too, Bill."

"Well, of course," Cody said. "We're two of a kind. Did you see Luke Short while you were in Fort Worth?"

"I did, indeed," Clint said. "He's watching my horse for me while I'm here."

"The horse Barnum gave you?"

"That's the one."

Cody speared a hunk of beef with his fork and then used it to point at Clint.

"You know, if I could get you and Luke and Bat Masterson in my show, we could all make a fortune."

"I'll make you a deal."

"What kind of deal?"

"If you get both Luke and Bat to say yes, you can count on me, as well."

Cody stared at Clint, and then burst out laughing.

"You're so damned sure they'd both say no, aren't you?" he asked.

"I'm positive."

"Don't be too positive," Cody said. "Remember, I got Hickok up on stage once."

"And he hated it."

"Yes, he did." Cody's face took on a nostalgic look. "He was quite a man, James Butler Hickok was."

"Yes, he was," Clint said. Their beer came at that moment and Clint lifted his in a toast. "To Wild Bill Hickok!"

"I'll sure as hell drink to that!" Cody said, and they clinked mugs.

NINE

"Before you make me an offer I can refuse," Clint said, "I've got some questions I want to ask you."

"Fire away."

"I know you had dinner with Annie Oakley last night and made her an offer."

"How do you know that?"

"Because I saw Annie and Frank both yesterday and this morning, Bill."

Cody sat back in his chair with a quizzical look on his face. "Are you folks gangin' up on me?" he asked.

"Not at all," Clint said. "In fact, I'm actually here in New York because of a telegram they sent me, not the one you sent me."

"They sent you a telegram? About what?"

"Seems they're having some trouble with a man who's threatening Annie."

"What?" Cody asked. "Why didn't she tell me about this last night?"

"Because you and she were doing business," Clint said. "This is a personal matter."

"If she's bein' threatened," Cody said, "I'd put business aside to help her. She knows it, Frank knows it, and you know it, Clint."

"I do know it, Bill," Clint said, "but for whatever reasons, they've asked me for help."

Cody mulled that over a moment, then shrugged and picked up his knife and fork again.

"I suppose if they couldn't come to me," he muttered, "you'd be the next best thing."

"Thanks a lot."

"You know what I mean," Cody said. "They couldn't have anybody better helpin' them. So what's it about?"

"Let me finish with my questions first," Clint said.

"Okay, go ahead."

"You wouldn't be trying to pull a fast one, would you, Bill?" he asked.

"Like what?"

"Like trying to put some pressure on Annie so she'll sign with you again?"

"You think I'd have somebody threaten her for that reason?"

"I'm just asking," Clint said. "This fella has been following her around the city—"

"Was he followin' her last night?" Cody demanded. "Blast it, man, I could have taken care of this—"

"No," Clint said. "He only follows her when she's alone."

"Look," Cody said, "why doesn't her husband take care of this for her? Why did he have to send for you?"

"Bill," Clint said, "you know as well as I do that Frank Butler is a trick shooter, a showman, not a gunman. He couldn't handle this fella himself. In fact, he tried."

"He did?" Cody asked, surprised. "Well, I give the lad points for that, then."

"But it didn't work," Clint said, "so they asked me to step in."

"And what have you done so far?"

"I met Annie, which I'd never done before," Clint said, "and it seems I've acquired a tail of my own."

"Did he follow you here?"

"He did."

Cody put down his knife and fork.

"Well, come on, man," he said. "Let's go out and shake some truth out of him, find out what's going on."

"Settle back down, Bill, and eat your steak," Clint said. "I'm going to take care of it myself. I just wanted to make sure you weren't trying to pull a fast one on anybody."

"Not me," Cody said. "I'm on the up and up, Clint. I'm trying to sign Annie, but I wouldn't scare her to try and get her."

"Okay," Clint said, "I accept that."

"So, you're gonna take care of this matter for them?"

"I am."

Somewhat mollified, Cody nodded and then said, "Then I guess we can talk about our business."

"Sure," Clint said, "go ahead."

"I suppose you know the offer I made Annie."

"I know you made an offer," Clint said. "I don't know any specific numbers."

"Well, here's the deal," he said. "You and she would be an unbeatable combination."

"What about her and Frank?"

"Everybody's seen them together," Cody said. "Everyone knows she can beat him. They don't know if she can beat you. This would be brand new."

"Bill—"

"Let me finish," Cody said. "One season, here on Staten Island. After that I'm goin' back to Europe. They love me over there. I'm tryin' to get some new acts to take back there with me, but if you both don't want to go, I won't hassle you. But if you'll work together for the next year here, it sure would be a boost to my show."

"Your show needs a boost, Bill?"

"The show always needs a boost, Clint," Cody said. "I'm gonna give you a number, and then you can talk. Okay?"

"Okay."

Cody gave him the number. Annie had been right. It was a big one.

TEN

"No," Clint said.

Cody looked across the table at him with great disappointment.

"Don't you even want to think about it?"

"No."

"Did you hear the number I quoted you?"

"Yes."

"Oh, good," Cody said, "I thought you were just gonna say no to everything I said."

"Not everything."

"Why are you so against workin' for me?" Cody asked. "How many times have I asked you, and you always say no."

"Three."

Cody looked surprised. "That's all?" he asked. "I thought it was more."

Clint thought a moment, then said, "No, it's three."

"Well heck," Cody said, "I got a few more in me, then. I'll go back to work tomorrow and look at the numbers; maybe I can sweeten the pot a little."

"Sweeten it all you want," Clint said. "I'm not about to spend a year of my life on Staten Island."

"You would live here, in Manhattan," Cody said. "I would get you a room in a nice residential hotel on Astor Place. You'd only have to come out to Staten Island to work. How does that sound?"

"Same answer as before."

"You try my patience, lad," Cody said, shaking his head.

"Maybe you'll stop asking, then."

"I'll come up with some new numbers."

"What about Annie's number?" Clint asked. "Will you sweeten that one, too?"

Cody's eyebrows went up as something new occurred to him. "You know, Annie and Frank need money," he said. "You know what they've been doin'? Shootin' matches in places like Trenton, New Jersey, and in Philadelphia. She was in a play in a theater on Fourteenth Street. Good God, man, she's not an actress, she's a headliner!"

"So sign them both up," Clint said.

Cody frowned. "Frank and I don't see eye to eye at times on what Annie should be doin'."

"He's her husband," Clint said. "He wants the best for her."

Cody pushed away the remnants of his meal and said, "I want a real drink. You?"

"Another beer is fine."

"And we have a guest joining us—as soon as he gets here." Cody turned in his seat, as Clint had the chair facing the front door. Right at that moment a man entered and Cody waved to him. "You know Nate, don't you, Clint?"

Clint stood up and shook hands with a man named Nate Salsbury. Nate was as shrewd as he was pleasant looking, and it was he who had convinced Bill Cody to go whole hog into the entertainment business instead of halfheartedly, giving rise to Buffalo Bill's Wild West Show as it now existed.

"Nice to see you, Clint," Nate said.

"I invited Nate to have a drink with us," Cody said. "Pull up a chair, Nate."

"What about Catlin?" Clint asked.

George Catlin was one of the first Wild West showmen who had joined forces with Cody after Salsbury came into the plainsman's life. Cody and Catlin were virtually partners, and it was the idea of both men to put Cody's name on the show, since he was the man with the reputation that would draw people.

"Catlin stays pretty much in the background these days," Cody said. "Nate and I run things."

Clint knew that the day-to-day business was run by the younger Salsbury, mainly because Cody had little patience for the mundane.

"Did the Colonel make his offer?" Nate asked.

"He did."

"And did you refuse it?"

"I did."

Nate looked at Cody and said, "See?"

"He turned me down the first time," Cody said. "I'm

getting another proposal ready even as we speak."

"Nate," Clint said, "can't you convince him to make an offer to Annie and Frank?"

"Annie's beaten Frank many times, Clint," Nate said. "Everybody knows that. She's also beaten Miles Johnson, Fred Kell, Bogardus, all of 'em. The only one she hasn't beaten is you."

The waiter came over and took drink orders from them, whiskey for Cody and Salsbury, another beer for Clint.

"Oh hell," he said at the last minute, "bring me a whiskey, too." He usually stayed away from whiskey, but it had been a fine meal and he thought it would be a good compliment to the good beer.

"Good," Cody said, "maybe we can get you drunk enough to sign right here and now."

Clint looked surprised. "You have a contract on you?"

"Of course," Cody said. He produced it from inside his buckskin jacket. "Want to see it?"

"No," Clint said, "thanks."

"I told you he wouldn't sign, Colonel," Nate said.

Cody tucked the contract away inside his jacket again and said, "Luckily, I don't give up as easily as you do, Nate."

Nate and Clint exchanged a glance and then the waiter appeared with their drinks.

ELEVEN

Abruptly, Cody announced he had to leave.

"You and Nate stay here and talk, Clint," he said, standing up. "I'll arrange for the bill to be taken care of."

"Bill—"

Cody cut him off by pointing a finger at him. "Whether you agree to sign with us or not, I want you to at least come out to Staten Island and look us over. I insist."

"Sure," Clint said, "I'll come and take a look—"

"You and Annie and Frank, come together," Cody said. "I'll arrange for lunch. How about tomorrow?"

"I'll ask them," Clint promised.

"Look," Cody said, "I know how tired Annie was in Europe, and homesick. But she's been back awhile now, she's worked for some other penny ante shows and she's shot matches. I think she's ready to come back."

"You might be right," Clint said, "but maybe she's not ready to come back without Frank."

Cody leaned forward and said, "Toward the end, in Germany, do you know what Frank was doin' in the show? He was throwin' her targets for her. Is that anythin' for a man to be doin'?"

"Maybe he loves her enough to do it."

Cody straightened up. "I'll see the three of you for lunch on Staten Island tomorrow, around twelve."

"Like I said," Clint replied, "I'll ask them."

"Fine. I'll see you then, though, with or without them."

Without waiting for an answer from Clint, Cody turned and left the restaurant. If he had made arrangements for the bill to be paid, Clint hadn't seen it.

"I could use some coffee," Nate said, and turned to wave to the waiter. When he turned back, he said, "Clint, you don't have to stay."

"He hasn't changed a bit, has he?" Clint asked.

"Why would he want to?" Nate asked. "It all works for him. He gets what he wants."

"Maybe not this time."

Nate smiled and said, "You know what? That would be a refreshing change."

"Are you supposed to convince me now?"

"That's what he hoped," Nate said, "but you know what? I'm not even gonna try. See, I believe you when you say you're not gonna sign. I don't think throwing more money at you is gonna change your mind."

"Thanks for that, Nate," Clint said. "It's not about the money for me. It's about not being a performing monkey."

"Hey, you don't have to convince me," Nate Salsbury

said. "I wouldn't want to get up and perform in front of thousands of people."

"Thousands?"

"Those were the crowds we were playing to in London and France and Germany," Nate said. "I don't expect to draw those crowds on Staten Island."

"Why Staten Island?" Clint asked. "After all that time in Europe playing to big crowds."

"It's a good place to try out new acts," Nate said, "for some of us to rest without actually closing the show down."

"Does Cody need rest?"

"He doesn't think so," Nate said, "but I can see it."

"I couldn't," Clint said, "not tonight. His energy was bouncing off the walls."

"Yeah, well," Nate said, "he left because he was exhausted. Within the next few minutes he'll be fast asleep in his hotel room."

"How's his health?"

"Oh, he's fine," Nate said. "He's not sick; he's just tired."

"What was that about Annie needing rest?"

"She was worn out in Europe," Nate said, "worn out and homesick. From what I heard she came back here and didn't work for two months. Kept her guns in a trunk. When she finally pulled them out, she and Frank went to work for some low-rent outfits. They finally came back here, and—in my opinion—they were waiting for us to get back. Took some shooting matches and did some theater work in the meantime, but they're ready to come back."

"So why won't Cody make an offer to Frank?"

"He thinks Frank could have gotten Annie to stay in

Europe," Nate said. "She could have got some rest there. Maybe stayed in Germany and then joined us in France. We did five weeks in France. He feels she could have worked two or three of those. Her leaving cut into our revenue, and he knows that Frank makes the financial decisions."

"Then why isn't he talking to Frank about Annie?"

"He will," Nate said. "He's gonna have to. That's what Annie told him last night, that she doesn't make the decisions."

"Well," Clint said, "she and Frank have a lot on their minds."

"Like what?"

Fresh coffee came and Nate poured it out for the two of them before Clint answered. He told Nate about Vernon Weeks and what he had been putting Annie through.

"So that's why you're here?" Nate asked. "To put a stop to it?"

"If I can."

"I don't see why you couldn't," Nate said. "Why wouldn't the guy just run when he finds out you're here?"

"That's a nice thought," Clint said, shaking his head, "but believe it or not, Nate, most men don't run away from me, they run at me."

Nate Salsbury shook his head and said, "It must be hard being you, sometimes."

Clint didn't comment.

TWELVE

Clint was about to suggest that they leave—or that he was leaving—when across the room he spotted a woman who was dining alone, and looking his way. Nate noticed his glance and followed it.

"Oh, my!" he said.

"I know."

"She's lookin' at you."

"I know."

"I have never seen hair that black combined with skin that white," Nate said.

"I know."

"And she looks like she's been painted by Rubens."

"I—" Clint started, then stopped because he was sounding monotonous even to himself.

"And she's alone."

"I noticed."

Nate turned around and picked up his coffee.

"You can go," he said. "I'll be fine."

"You haven't made your pitch."

"I told you I wouldn't," Nate said. "All you have to do is tell the Colonel I did."

"It's a deal. Where's that waiter?"

All he had to do was wave and the man appeared.

"What is that lady drinking?" Clint asked.

The waiter didn't have to ask "What lady?" because every man in the place was looking at her. Clint thought he must be getting old for not having noticed her before.

"That's Mrs. Walker," the waiter said, "and she drinks champagne, usually."

"Well, bring her a bottle and let her know it's from me, will you?" Clint asked.

"Yes, sir," the man said. "Shall I mention a name?"

"Clint Adams."

"Very well, sir."

"If you don't mind," Nate said, "I'll stay around until you make the walk over there. I can live vicariously through you."

"Maybe I'll be making the long walk back, too."

"Have you changed since I saw you last?"

"Not much."

"Then not much chance of that, is there?" Nate asked. "Especially considering the hot glances she keeps sending over here."

"She could be looking at you."

"Clint," Nate said, "a beautiful woman has never looked at me like that, and one is not about to start now. On second thought, I think I'll leave before you walk over there. The envy might kill me."

Salsbury stood up and shook hands with Clint.

"It was good to see you," he said.

"Will you be on Staten Island tomorrow?"

"You know," Nate said, "there's really very little call for me to go out there. I mean, that's where all the performing is done. Most of my work is done here in the city. So, no, I probably won't see you tomorrow."

Nate saw the waiter walking across the floor toward Mrs. Walker with a bottle of champagne.

"I better go. Good night, Clint . . . and good luck."

"Night, Nate."

Nate left as the waiter reached the woman's table with the bottle of champagne. Clint watched as the waiter pointed to him and spoke to the woman, who seemed very pleased. As the waiter made to open the champagne, Clint began to get up, but the woman stopped them both with a gesture. She stood up, took the bottle from the waiter and walked across the floor to Clint's table. She was wearing a long blue dress, cut rather low in front to reveal an amazing cleavage that seemed to undulate as she approached him.

"I believe," she said when she reached his table, "we should share this, don't you?"

THIRTEEN

Her name was Karyn Walker, and Clint doubted that he had ever seen a woman with such opulent curves. She was a large woman, but every curve was in its proper proportion. As she disrobed in his room, Clint thought about Nate Salsbury's words before he left the restaurant. He, too, had never seen a woman with such black hair and white skin, and now all that skin—every luscious, bountiful curve of it—was fully in view for him. In addition, the hair between her ripe thighs was as black as the hair on her lovely head.

Completely naked, she was every man's dream. Her breasts were large and pendulous, swaying as she walked toward him. Her nipples were dark brown, with large, rather oval aureole rather than round. Clint found himself captivated by the sight of them as she came closer, and

rather inanely he realized at that moment that he knew
nothing about this woman beyond the fact that she was
naked and in his room . . .

They had shared the bottle of champagne at the restaurant,
but their conversation had been small talk rather than in-
formative. She seemed unwilling to share very much information about herself, and so Clint supplied little
beyond his name.

She, however, had some questions for him that she
would not allow to go unanswered.

"Was that Buffalo Bill Cody I saw you dining with?"
she asked.

"Yes, it was," Clint said. "He's . . . a friend of mine."

"That would make you a rather important man,
wouldn't it?" she asked.

She had a lovely face, with big brown eyes and full
lips, but he was finding it hard to keep his eyes off the
deep valley between her breasts.

"No," he said, "Colonel Cody is an important man. I'm
just a friend of his."

"How do you know him?"

"Our paths have crossed here and there."

"Not here," she said, "in the East."

"Why do you say that?" he asked.

"Because you don't belong here," she said. "It's obvious. You don't belong in that suit."

He sat back and shrugged his shoulders. "It doesn't
fit?"

"Oh, it fits fine," she said. "I just think you'd be more
comfortable in something more . . . informal."

"That's funny," he said, "I was just thinking the same
thing about you."

She continued to ask him questions about himself, even as she sidestepped questions he fired back. They left the restaurant and he took her to the Waldorf and into the bar, where she was the only woman. He could hear the jaws of all the men in the place—the lobby as well as the bar— as they dropped, and took great pride in the fact that she was with him.

After a few drinks in the Waldorf bar, Karyn finally mentioned how she'd like to get a look at a Waldorf room—preferably Clint's. Still knowing virtually nothing about the woman, he took her to his room . . .

Their first kiss took place with both of them fully clothed, but he could feel the heat of her body as she molded herself to him.

"This is just for tonight," she whispered into his ear, her breath hot. "It's important that you understand that."

"All right."

"And no more questions," she said, "no more talk. Agreed?"

"Agreed."

That was when she backed up and began to disrobe, until she was standing naked in front of him, and then against him.

He slid his hands down her smooth back until he reached her buttocks. Gripping them, kneading them, he kissed her again, a deep, devouring kiss. She pressed her groin to his and felt how hard he was, so she broke the kiss and got down on her knees. He allowed her to remove his boots and trousers and underwear, and then his rigid penis was in her hands, between her lush breasts and, finally, in her mouth. He took off his shirt and then, naked, spread his feet apart and took hold of her head with his hands.

She sucked him until he was ready to burst, then stopped, stood and kissed him again. Her naked breasts felt hot and heavy against his chest, her nipples as hard as small stones. He let his hands roam over her body while they kissed, and then they fell onto the bed, still locked together.

He was so fascinated by the fullness of her body that he rolled her over onto her back so he could explore her at will. First he looked at her, took in the lushness of her as her breasts flattened yet seemed to grow rounder. Then he took them in his hands, brought them together and kissed them, first the aureole around the nipples, and then the nipples themselves. She cupped his head and held him to her chest, moaning as he started to suck and bite her. He slid one hand down over her belly and delved into the tangled forest of hair there until he found her, wet and waiting. He slid his finger up and down the length of her moist slit and then let it slip inside of her. She lifted her butt off the bed and pressed it against his hand, moaned into his mouth as he kissed her. He moved his mouth to her neck and shoulders and then back to the slopes of her breasts. He couldn't remember the last time he had encountered such soft, smooth, fragrant flesh.

He moved down her body then, kissing her nipples, her flesh beneath her breasts, her belly—pausing for a few moments to toil over her deep navel—and then finally, he explored her with his mouth and tongue until her body was as taut as a bowstring and she was begging him to both stop and never stop . . .

Eventually, however, he did stop, but only because his own excitement was getting the better of him. His erection felt as if it was going to burst, and he wanted nothing more at that moment than to bury it inside of her. He slid up her body, spread her legs with his knees and drove himself into her. She gasped and brought her legs up around him, and he fucked her and kissed her at the same time, so that when she cried out it was into his mouth.

He slid his hands beneath her to cup her succulent buttocks and lift her up to meet each of his strokes. Her breath, when he wasn't smothering her with kisses, came hard and raspy in his ear and then she began to whisper to him, "Oh God, oh yes, oh Jesus," but louder and louder, so that eventually she was whispering no more, but yelling. If they had been in a cheaper hotel with thinner walls, everyone would have heard them, because when his time came, he opened his mouth and bellowed like a bull, and then suddenly they were laughing and clutching each other with pleasure and relief . . .

FOURTEEN

They awoke several times during the night and did it over again, and then repeated the process in the morning. Finally, spent and sweating, they rolled apart and tried to catch their breath.

"I smell like a goat," she said, laughing. "May I take a bath before I leave?"

He suspected she needed the bath so she could go home to her husband without smelling like she'd spent the night having sex. He wondered idly where and with whom Mr. Walker thought she was spending the night.

"Of course," he said. "It's through there. I can draw it for you, if you like."

"Oh, no," she said, rising from the bed, "if I let you into that room with me, we won't come out until this afternoon."

He eyed her opulent flesh as she walked across to the door. The odor she was giving off was very ungoatlike, and the smell combined with the sight of her was making him hard again.

"Would that be so bad?"

She looked at him over her shoulder, saw him staring directly at her majestic ass, and said, "That constitutes a question. We agreed last night, when we entered this room—no questions."

"Sorry."

She blew him a kiss and went in to take a bath, taking her clothing from the night before with her.

When she came out, she was as lovely looking and smelling as she had been the night before. The hellcat he'd been in bed with all night was gone, replaced by this beautiful lady.

"Last night was wonderful," she said, coming to the bed and kissing him briefly.

"I agree," he said. "Thank you."

She went to the door and opened it.

"If you ever want to get a look at the inside of a Waldorf room again . . . ," he said.

"I'll remember," she said. She started to leave, then stopped and turned to look at him. "How long will you be here?"

"The rest of the week, at least," he said, "maybe more."

She gave that some thought, then said, "We'll see," and left.

He laid back with his hands clasped behind his bed and took a moment to recall everything that had happened the night before. He was in danger of drifting off to sleep again—not that he'd gotten that much sleep during the night—when he remembered he had to be at Frank and Annie's hotel by nine.

He got up and went to take a bath himself, before going down to breakfast.

It was his second breakfast in the Waldorf's dining room, but the waiter already knew what he wanted.

"Steak and eggs this morning, Mr. Adams?" he asked.

"You remembered, Richard."

"Always remember the good tippers, Mr. Adams," Richard said, "and the famous people. You happen to be both."

This was the first inkling Clint had that the waiter had recognized his name.

"Coffee comin' up," the young man promised.

Clint sat back in his chair. During the cab drive from the restaurant back to the Waldorf last night, with Karyn Walker pressed tightly against him, he hadn't given much thought to the man who had followed him there. He wondered if the tail had tried to follow them back on foot, before realizing where they were headed.

He wondered if the man was outside now, waiting for him to come out. Or if he'd followed Karyn Walker home. Wouldn't that be embarrassing for her with her husband if she were somehow drawn into this whole thing. Clint hoped that the man had shown no interest in her and had let her go home on her own.

Richard came with the coffee and Clint allowed him to pour him a cup.

"Thank you, Richard."

"A newspaper, Mr. Adams?"

"What have you got?"

"How about the *Morning Telegraph*?"

"Why not?" Clint asked.

"Comin' up."

The newspaper came before his breakfast, but the steak and eggs did follow soon after, and he read the paper while he ate. There was little in the way of local news that interested him, unless you included the fact that New York State had just instituted electrocution as a method of execution. In addition, someone seemed to have just patented something called an adding machine.

He put the paper down and finished his excellent steak-and-egg breakfast, then polished off the rolls with another pot of coffee. Remembering that he had already been touted as an "excellent tipper," he left Richard a sizeable one, then left the hotel to go and follow Annie for the day.

FIFTEEN

Clint's own tail was still on him, a rather disheveled man he was going to have to do something about sooner or later. He didn't know if the man's job was simply to follow him, or if there was going to be an attempt on his life at some point. By the end of the day he was going to have to find out.

Annie and Frank Butler's hotel was near Madison Square. Clint decided to take a cab there, if just to give the man following him a hard time.

When he arrived at the hotel he looked around to see if either his tail or Annie's was around. He picked out a nice doorway for himself across the street and positioned himself there. He was very early, but he wanted to study the area for a while, see where a man might secret himself to await Annie's appearance. He saw the lamppost on the corner where Frank had probably had his encounter with Vernon Weeks.

After an hour or so there was still no sight of Weeks or anyone else. He looked at the windows of the buildings across from him, and wondered if Weeks might not be in one of the buildings on his side of the street, looking out a window.

Another half hour and Annie would make her appearance. He loosened the Colt New Line in his belt, and folded his arms to wait.

Annie Oakley stared out her window, gnawing on a fingernail as she did.

"That better not be your trigger finger," Butler said, from behind her. "That's much too valuable a digit for you to be biting."

She pulled the finger away from her mouth and folded her arms.

"I don't see Clint."

"That's the idea," Butler said. "You don't see Clint, and neither does Vernon Weeks."

"I don't see Weeks, either," she said, worriedly.

"Maybe he's seen Clint already and he's decided to go away."

"But he would come back," she said. "What's the point of having Clint here if Weeks is not going to be here?"

Butler came up behind her and put his hands on her shoulders.

"It's five minutes to nine," he said. "Clint is waiting for you out there."

"I hope he is."

He patted her shoulders now and said, "He is. Go on.

I'll watch from here, and I bet I'll see him fall in behind you."

She went to put on her vest, then checked the derringer she'd put in the pocket the night before without telling Butler.

"Okay, I'm ready."

Butler gave her a hug and a kiss and sent her out the door, hoping he was doing the right thing.

When Annie came out the front door, Clint could sense her tension from across the street. She paused just outside the door and looked around, very obviously searching for either him or Vernon Weeks. She didn't spot either, and eventually just started walking up the street. Clint waited, watching from his doorway to see if anyone started after her. When no one did, he stepped out and began trailing her himself.

He already knew this wasn't going to work.

Vernon Weeks watched the street from the window, and eventually saw Annie Oakley come out of the hotel. She paused, then started walking. From his vantage point Wells could not see his side of the street, but he leaned out to see as much as he could and was rewarded when he saw Clint Adams start walking about a block behind Annie.

Did he think it would be this easy? Vernon wondered.

Clint followed Annie for a few hours as she stopped in stores, bought nothing, came out, looked around, then moved on to the next one. Finally, as she went into one store, he closed the gap between them and went in after her.

"Clint!" she said, surprised to see him. "W-what are you doing here? Did you see him?"

"This is not going to work, Annie," he said. "Somehow he knew I was here, and he's not following you."

"B-but maybe you just can't see him."

"I don't think he's that good," Clint said. "I don't think anybody's that good."

"So . . . what do we do now?"

"Well," he said, "it's about time for lunch, I think, unless you had other plans."

"The only plans I had were for you to follow me and get Vernon Wells out of my life," she said.

He thought for a moment she was going to lose control, and had to admire her for taking charge of herself again before that could happen.

"Since that plan is shot to hell," she said, "lunch sounds like a good alternative—but I get to pick the place."

"Agreed," he said.

SIXTEEN

She took him to a restaurant down on Printer's Row, where most of the newspapers and publishers had their offices.

"After lunch we can walk down to the Brooklyn Bridge," she said, as they were seated in the small café.

"I was here when it was opened," he told her, "but I haven't seen it since then. I guess it's still standing, then?"

"Oh, yes," she said, her eyes shining, "it's a marvel! But if you've already seen it—"

"No, no," he said, "I'll look forward to seeing it."

"We could even walk over it!" she said, excitedly. She was extraordinarily pretty, with the enthusiasm of a little girl—when she wasn't being followed or threatened.

A waitress came and took their order, and brought coffee for him and lemonade for her.

"I feel guilty now," she said.

"Why?"

"We're havin' a nice lunch and Frank is back at the hotel, worrying about me."

"He'll get over it," Clint said. "I had dinner with Cody last night."

"I forgot to ask," she said. "How did it go? Did he throw a lot of money at you?"

"Yes, he did."

"And what did you say?"

"I said no."

"He must have had a fit."

"He brought in the cavalry."

"Nate?"

"Yes," Clint said, "but it didn't do any—Oh, wait."

"What is it?"

"He said he wanted the three of us out on Staten Island for lunch," Clint said. "I completely forgot." With all the excitement last night with Karyn, and then today following Annie, the invitation—or command—had completely slipped his mind.

"Good."

"Good that I forgot?"

"Yes," she said. "He has to see that he doesn't always get what he wants."

"He didn't have a fit last night," Clint said, "but he's sure gonna have one today."

"He'll get over it," she said. "And we'll go and have lunch with him tomorrow. Just now we're having a nice lunch right here."

And that's what they did.

• • •

The food Clint had had so far in New York had all been good—as was usually the case when he was there—and the little café on Printer's Row was no exception. Just as they were leaving, it started to fill up with the people from the publishing houses and newspapers.

"We got out just in time," Annie said. "Still want to walk to the bridge?"

"Let's do it."

They started walking downtown, her arm linked in his.

"My goodness," she said, her free hand suddenly going to her mouth.

"What is it?"

"I totally forgot to look around for Vernon Weeks."

"Don't worry," he said, "I did, and he's not there."

"But . . . I mean, I didn't even think about it."

"That's a good thing, Annie."

"I guess I . . . I just feel safe with you."

"Another good thing."

"But . . . I could never tell Frank that," she said. "It would break his heart. He's feelin' bad enough about himself already."

"Okay, then," Clint said, patting her hand, "it'll be our secret."

They walked down to the bridge and stood there staring at it as it spanned the East River from Manhattan to Brooklyn.

"That is just amazing," she said. "I can't believe it."

He couldn't, either, and he had been there the day it opened with great fanfare. He recalled wondering if the thing would stand, or fall in on itself. Apparently, it was standing.

"Let's walk across," she said excitedly.

"All right."

As they walked, still arm in arm, she said, "He's right, you know."

"Who's right?"

"Cody."

"About what?"

"About you and me being a big draw."

"You're already a big draw."

"A bigger one with you, though."

He hesitated a moment, then asked, "Are you telling me you'd like me to do it?"

"Oh, no," she said, squeezing his arm. "I don't want you to do anything you don't want to do. I'm just sayin'. . . Cody's a genius. Most of the ideas he comes up with work. This one would, too."

"I don't doubt it," Clint said, "but the simple fact of the matter is, I don't want to be put on display."

"And the simple fact of the matter for me is," she replied, "I do. I guess that's the big difference between us."

There were more differences than that, Clint thought, but he didn't bother pointing them out at that moment.

SEVENTEEN

Frank Butler left the hotel soon after his wife did. He decided to take advantage of the afternoon alone and do some shopping. He didn't know when their next job would be, but he needed some new shirts and maybe a new hat.

He came out of the hotel and turned left. He didn't bother to look around for any sign of Vernon Weeks, because he assumed—and hoped—that the man had followed Annie, so Clint Adams could get his hands on him.

As it turned out, he would have saved himself a lot of trouble if he'd looked behind himself, just once.

Vernon Weeks stepped out of the doorway he'd been standing in, just next to Frank Butler's hotel. He marveled at the fact that the man did not look behind him, even

75

once. Weeks followed him to the corner, and around onto
a side street.

He had no idea where Frank Butler was going, but he
knew for a fact that he was not going to get there.

Clint and Annie walked on the Brooklyn Bridge, but did
not go all the way to Brooklyn. Instead, they stopped halfway to admire the view and then turned back.

It was late afternoon when they reached the Manhattan
side again and Clint asked, "Would you like to get a drink
somewhere?"

"I'm really not much of a drinker, Clint," she said. "I
think I'd just like to go back to the hotel."

"I'll get you a cab and ride along with you."

"You don't have to do that—"

"Just because Weeks didn't follow you today doesn't
mean he won't be waiting for you back at the hotel."

Her eyes widened and she said, "Well, if you put it
that way, all right. I accept."

Frank Butler had already picked out a favorite store for
clothes while he and Annie were in New York, and he
liked to walk there. It was on Broadway, a street he found
very much to his liking. He usually used an alley between
Sixth Avenue and Broadway to get there, and today was
no different—except for the footsteps he suddenly heard
behind him.

He started to turn and heard somebody say, "Nighty
night, Frank," before everything went dark.

Clint and Annie stepped down from a cab in front of her
hotel. Annie looked around the area while Clint paid the
driver.

"I don't see anyone," she said.

Clint looked also, then raised his eyes and looked across the street. There were plenty of windows, but none of the buildings was a hotel. Still, it wouldn't be hard to get into a building across the street to make use of a window. He'd have to check it out.

"What are you lookin' at?" Annie asked.

"I'm just thinking about something," he said. "Come on, I'll walk you to your room and say hello to Frank. We better make some plans to go out and see Cody, tomorrow."

"Oh, right," she said. "I forgot about that."

She took his arm and they entered the hotel together.

Annie fitted her key into the lock and opened the door. It was a residential hotel that was a far cry from the Waldorf. Clint felt bad that Annie and Frank Butler didn't have the money to stay in a better place. It seemed to him Annie should be accepting Cody's offer, whether Butler was included or not. Of course, that was up to them . . .

"Frank?" she called as she entered.

It was one room, and rather cramped for two people—unless, of course, they loved each other.

"He's not here," she said. "He didn't tell me he was gonna go out anywhere."

Clint could see by the expression on Annie's face that she was worried.

"Let me go downstairs and talk to the desk clerk," he said. "Maybe he saw him leave."

"All right," she said, "but hurry back, please. I have a bad feeling about this."

"I'll be right back."

The clerk was a sleepy-looking man in his thirties who seemed startled when Clint approached the desk.

"Can I help ya?"

"Do you know Mr. and Mrs. Butler, in room seventeen?"

"You mean the Oakleys?"

"I mean the Butlers," Clint said. "Annie Oakley and her husband, Frank Butler."

The man shrugged and said, "Okay, yeah, whatever you wanna call 'em. I know them."

"Did you see him leave this morning?"

"Afternoon, more likely," the man said, "but yeah, I did."

"Did he say where he was going?"

"He waved at me and said somethin' about goin' ta get a new hat, or a shirt, or somethin'."

"And how long ago was that?"

"Few hours, I guess."

"Okay, thanks."

Clint went back upstairs and gave Annie the news.

"He did say he was gonna buy some new clothes," she said. "He's picked out some favorite stores while we've been here."

"Do you want to go out and look for him in some of them?" Clint asked.

"I don't know where they all are, Clint," she said. "I think I'll just wait here."

"Well, all right—"

"Would you wait with me?" She grabbed his arm. "I'm really scared something's happened to him."

"Of course I'll stay with you, Annie," he said. "He'll probably be here any minute."

Annie released his arm and walked to the window, where she stood, hugging herself.

"I hope you're right."

EIGHTEEN

As it grew darker out, Annie's mood grew darker, as well.

"It's Weeks," she said, "I know it. He did somethin' to Frank."

"Let's not jump to conclusions, Annie," Clint said. "Maybe he got carried away with his shopping. After all, he expected you to be with me, and he expected Weeks to be following you."

"No," she said, turning away from the window. "He wouldn't stay away this long, not when he knows what we've been going through. He's just not that thoughtless."

Clint didn't say so, but he felt the same way. Frank Butler was not the type of man who would worry his wife this way.

"Maybe I should go and look—" he started, but just then there was a knock at the door.

"Maybe he forgot his key," Clint said, but he could see by the look on Annie's face that she didn't believe that, and he didn't, either.

"Would you get that, Clint?" she asked. "I can't seem to move from this spot."

Clint went to the door and opened it, and found himself facing a uniformed policeman.

"Is this where Annie Oakley lives?" he asked. He was young, and his voice cracked when he said Annie's name.

"Yes," Clint said. "She's right here." He stepped back to let the policeman enter.

"Are you Annie Oakley?"

"I am."

"And you're married to Frank Butler?"

"Y-yes." This time Annie's voice cracked. Clint moved quickly to her side, because if the policeman said Frank was dead he knew he'd have to hold her up.

"What's this about, Officer?" Clint asked.

"Who are you, sir?"

"My name is Clint Adams."

"H-He's a friend. Can you tell me, has something happened to my husband?"

"He's in the hospital, ma'am."

She covered her face with her hands.

"Is he alive?" Clint asked.

"Yes, sir, he is," the policeman said, "but he's been injured. He was found in an alley over near Broadway."

"What happened to him?"

"If you would both come with me, Lieutenant Egan can tell you all about it."

"Egan?" Clint asked.

"Yes, sir."

Clint looked at Annie. "I know the lieutenant."

"Are you . . . friends?" the policeman asked.

"I wouldn't say that," Clint said. "I don't think Lieutenant Egan has any friends."

"Sounds like you know him," the officer said with a smile, but he quickly wiped it away. "Ma'am? I have a buggy outside and can take you—both of you—to the hospital, if you like."

"Yes," Annie said, "please, right away."

"This way, then."

The officer allowed both Annie and Clint to precede him, then made sure to close the door to the room as he followed them out. Clint had the feeling the young man was smitten.

The policeman's name was Officer George Owens, he told them as he drove them to St. John's Hospital. When they arrived, he hastened to get down so he could help Annie out of the buggy.

"Thank you, Officer Owens."

"My pleasure, ma'am," he said. "If it's not out of line, ma'am, I've seen you shoot. You're the best I've ever seen."

"Well . . . thank you, Officer. I appreciate that."

"Lieutenant Egan should be just inside."

Owens led the way, and as they entered the lobby, Clint saw Egan talking to a doctor. The lieutenant's looks had not improved since he'd last seen him. He still looked like a man who slept in his clothes. When Egan spotted Clint, he frowned, then shook his head. He turned away from the doctor as Clint and Annie approached him.

"Now why doesn't this surprise me?" Lieutenant Egan asked.

NINETEEN

"Lieutenant," Clint said, "this is Annie Oakley."

Egan looked at her. "Miss Oakley—or do you prefer Mrs. Butler?"

"Mrs. Butler will do," she said. "Can I see my husband, please?"

"Of course," Lieutenant Egan said. "This is Dr. Davis. He's takin' care of your husband. He'll take you to his room and fill you in on his condition."

"Just follow me, Mrs. Butler."

"Can you fill *me* in on his condition, Lieutenant?" Clint asked.

"How long have you been in New York, Adams?"

"About two days."

"And already you're involved in something?"

"The Butlers are friends of mine."

"I suppose you know Cody, too."

"Yes, I do."

"Figures."

"Frank's condition, Lieutenant?"

"Somebody whacked him over the head with a gun butt," Egan said. "He'll live."

"Did he see who did it?"

"No," Egan said, "and that's the odd thing. He didn't see the man, but he claims to know who it was."

"Vernon Weeks?"

"Yeah, that's the name," Egan said. "What's goin' on?"

"This Weeks has apparently been following Mrs. Butler—Annie Oakley—stalking her, really," Clint said, "like some love-crazed fan or something."

"Well," Egan said, "that may be the case, but if he didn't see the man hit him, I can't arrest him—even if I could find him. Am I safe in assuming he'd be hard to find?"

"Very safe. Why did something like this bring you down here, Lieutenant?"

"Celebrities," he said. "I know Butler's name, knew he was married to Annie Oakley, knew they were friends of Cody. Didn't know you were involved, too, though."

"I'm just a friend who happened to be around," Clint said.

"You ain't tryin' to help them with this Weeks fella?"

"Well, maybe a bit . . ."

"That's what I thought," Egan said. "You carrying a gun on you now?"

"I might be."

"Mrs. Butler?"

"I can't speak for her."

Egan pointed a sausage-like finger at Clint.

"I ain't gonna search you now, Adams," he said, "but if you fire a shot while you're here, I'm gonna be all over you." Egan shook his head. "Last time it was P. T. Barnum, this time Annie Oakley and Buffalo Bill. Ain't you got any normal friends?" He didn't wait for an answer, just started to walk away.

"Lieutenant."

"What?" Egan stopped and turned.

"Are you going to put a guard on Frank's door?" Clint asked. "After all, somebody did attack him."

"It was probably just a robbery attempt—"

"Was anything taken?"

Egan paused, then said, "No."

"How about leaving us that young policeman—what's his name—Owens?"

"Fine," Egan said, "you can have him. I'll send him in. Anything else?"

Clint was going to ask for Frank Butler's room number, but he had watched the doctor lead Annie down a hallway. He decided just to go and look for himself.

"No," he said, "that'll be fine, thanks."

He found Annie standing by Frank Butler's bed, with the doctor on the other side. Butler had a bandage on his head, like a turban.

"Frank?" Clint said. "You okay?"

Butler looked at him as he entered the room.

"I'm fine," Butler said. "I told them I don't need to be here—and I don't need this." He pointed to the bandage.

"Frank, the doctor says you do," Annie argued.

"Just overnight, Mr. Butler," Dr. Davis said. "We just

want to make sure you're okay. We don't want you walking out of here and then collapsing on the street, do we?"

"No," Annie said, "we do not."

"Excuse me."

Clint turned and saw George Owens standing in the doorway.

"I'll just be standing out here for a while," Officer Owens said. "Just to make sure everything's okay."

"Thank you, Officer Owens," Annie said.

"Just doin' my job, ma'am."

"Another conquest, Annie?" Frank Butler asked.

"He's sweet on her, all right," Clint said. "You should have seen him rush to help her from the buggy."

"Stop it, you two. Did you arrange for that with your friend Lieutenant Egan, Clint?"

"The lieutenant and I aren't friends," Clint said, "but yes, I did arrange for Officer Owens to be on guard tonight."

"I'll check back with you later, Mr. Butler," Dr. Davis said, and left.

"It was Weeks, Clint," Butler said, right away.

"You didn't see him, though, did you?"

"No, but I heard him."

"He said something?"

"He said, 'Nighty night, Frank,' just before he hit me."

"That son of a bitch!" Annie swore. "We thought we were drawing him out for Clint to grab him, but he stayed behind to go after you."

"He's trying to show us he's in control," Clint said.

"Well, he is!" Annie said.

"Don't shout at Clint, Annie," Butler said. "It's not his fault."

"No, it's your fault for goin' out!" she snapped.

"What was I supposed to do, just stay inside like a prisoner?" Butler demanded.

"Uh, I'm going to wait outside with the young policeman . . . ," Clint said, but neither of the Butlers was listening to him, so he just slipped from the room.

TWENTY

Clint stood outside the room with Officer Owens, closing the door behind him.

"Are they fighting?" Owens asked.

"Oh, yeah."

"She's pretty great, you know," the young man said. Then he blushed and hurriedly added, "I mean, with a gun."

"I know what you mean."

"He's pretty good, too," Owens said, "but not near as good as she is."

"I know," Clint said. "You shoot?"

"Some."

"Any good?"

The young policeman inflated his chest. "I'm okay

with a handgun, but I'm a dead shot with a rifle," he said. "Oh, nothing like Annie Oakley—"

"—because she's special," Clint finished.

"Right."

"Got it."

"I know your reputation, sir."

"Do you?"

"Yes, sir," Owens said. "Very fast with a gun."

"So they tell me."

"Are you accurate?" Owens asked.

Clint turned his head and looked at the young man. They were standing on either side of the doorway.

"I mean, of course I've heard you're fast," Owens said, "but I never heard much about . . . you know, accuracy."

"I can generally hit what I shoot at."

"Clay pigeon?" Owens asked. "Real birds?"

"People," Clint said, deciding to see if he could shock the man.

"Sir?"

"I shoot at people," Clint said, again, then added, "Of course, when they shoot at me first."

"Oh," Owens said, "yes, I, uh, see . . ."

Officer Owens fell silent then, and a few moments later Annie Oakley came out of the room. Her face was flushed. She was either very angry, or they'd been doing something else in that room.

"Clint?"

"Yes."

"I'd like to go back to the hotel and get some clean clothes for Frank. Would you come with me?"

"Of course."

"I'll stay here," Officer Owens said, as if he had other options.

"Thank you, Officer Owens," Annie said, placing her hand on his arm. "I appreciate your help."

Owens blushed at the physical contact and said, "Just doin' my job, ma'am."

"Well, thank you anyway."

"Shall we go?" Clint asked her.

"Yes," she said. They started away; then she stopped, turned and said to Owens, "I'm sorry, where are my manners? Can we bring you anything when we come back?"

"Uh . . . I am kind of hungry."

"Of course. What would you like?"

"Oh, anything would be fine, ma'am," he said. "I'm not choosy about what I eat."

"We'll bring you something nice," she said, then turned to Clint and said, "Let's go."

Out in front of the hospital Annie stopped and began to shake.

"Are you all right?"

"No," she said. "I'm frightened and I'm angry."

"Angry at who?"

"At Vernon Weeks," she said, "at Frank because he's such a . . . a man sometimes."

"He'll be okay, Annie," Clint said. "He's safe where he is, with a policeman on the door."

"Yes, but he won't stay there," she said. "He wants to go back to the hotel."

Of course, Clint thought, that's why they were going to get him fresh clothes.

"Will he stay overnight?"

"Yes," she said, "I was able to convince him of that, but if we go and see Cody tomorrow, he wants to be with us."

"Cody," Clint said. "I keep forgetting about him."

Annie giggled suddenly, like a little girl, and covered her mouth with both hands.

"That would drive him crazy if he knew," she said. "He wants people to pay attention to him all the time, and to remember him."

"There must be some way we can get a message to him out on Staten Island."

"There's an easier way than that."

"What's that?"

"Send a message to his hotel."

"And where's that?"

She turned her head and looked at him. "He didn't tell you. He's in the same hotel you are, the Waldorf."

TWENTY-ONE

Clint took Annie back to her hotel to collect some clean clothes for Frank. The clothes he was brought in with were dirty and torn. Clint had the cab wait for them and, after that, had it take them over to the Waldorf to either speak with Cody, or leave him a message. The old Indian-Scout-turned-showman wasn't in, so they left him a message saying they would come out to Staten Island the next day, unless he left Clint a message to do otherwise. After that they took the cab back to the hospital.

"What the hell are you doin' here?"

The man jumped at the sound of the voice, then settled down when he saw Vernon Weeks.

"Don't do that," he said. "You scared me half to death."

"Why are you here?" Weeks asked.

"Adams is in there," he said, pointing to the hospital across the street.

"Why isn't he dead yet?"

"Well . . . I ain't had a clear shot."

"I thought this was something you wanted to do."

"It is," the man said, "I just been thinkin'."

"About what?"

"That maybe I could use some help."

"Look," Weeks said, "I'm payin' you to do a job. You wanna pay somebody else to help you, that's your business. It comes out of your money."

"I know," the man said, "but it would be worth it. So you don't care if I bring somebody in?"

"As long as it's not somebody who's gonna muck up the works," Weeks said. "Make sure it's somebody who will do exactly what they're told."

"He will."

"Unlike you."

"Hey—"

"Never mind," Weeks said.

"So what are you doin' here?"

"The girl with Adams is Annie Oakley," Weeks said. "Her husband's in there."

"He got hurt?"

"He did."

"How'd that happen?"

Weeks just looked at the man.

"Oh."

Annie had insisted that they stop at Gunther's restaurant to get something for Officer Owens.

"He's already halfway in love with you, Annie," Clint

told her. "If you bring him something to eat from here, you'll push him the rest of the way."

"He has to eat, so he might as well eat well."

When she handed the officer the wrapped up sandwich and he opened it, his eyes lit up.

"Is that a steak sandwich?" he asked.

"It's from the best place in town," she told him. "Enjoy."

"Thank you, Mrs. Butler—I mean, Miss Oakley—" the young man stammered.

"Officer Owens," she said, "you can just call me Annie. Okay?"

"A-all right . . . Annie."

She looked at Clint and said, "I'll just be a minute."

Clint waited in the hall with Owens while Annie took the change of clothes in to Frank and threatened him to make sure he stayed in the hospital overnight.

"I told you she was great," Owens said, happily munching on his steak sandwich.

"I know."

TWENTY-TWO

Vernon Weeks walked into the hospital bold as you please and asked about the condition of Frank Butler at the front desk.

"Are you a friend of his?" the fiftyish nurse on duty asked.

"A close friend."

She smiled and said, "He's doing very well. I heard the doctor say he would be released tomorrow morning."

"That's wonderful," Weeks said, with a pleasant smile. "What room is he in? I'd like to give him my best."

She leaned forward and said, "I shouldn't tell you this since the police were here, but you're such a good friend and all . . . He's right down that hall in room one thirteen."

Weeks touched her hand and said, "Thank you."

She blushed and said, "You're welcome."

Weeks started down the hall, saw the policeman on the door eating a sandwich, and then saw Clint Adams standing next to him. Abruptly, he turned and walked into room 109.

"Oops," he said to the old man in the bed, "wrong room."

"Hey," the man called, "stay and talk to me."

"Sorry, Pop," he said, "I got things to do."

"Everybody's got things to do," the old man complained as Weeks left, "that's why nobody's here talkin' to me."

Weeks left the old man's room and headed back the way he had come, up the hall and past the nurse.

"Did you get to see him?" the nurse asked, but Weeks just kept walking until he was out the door.

He rejoined the other man across the street.

"They've got a uniformed policeman on Butler's door," he said, "and The Gunsmith was there."

"So whatta we do?"

"You get out of here and go get your help," Weeks said. "We're not gonna get nothin' done here today."

"Okay," the man said.

"I'll be in touch."

The other man nodded, stepped from the doorway and turned left. Weeks gave him a head start, then stepped out himself and went to the right.

By the time Annie came out, she was red in the face again, and Owens was down to the last bite of his sandwich.

"That man is so frustrating," she said.

"Is he going to stay here tonight?" Clint asked.

"He says he will," she replied, "but who knows what he'll do as soon as we leave."

"I won't let him leave if you don't want him to, uh . . . Annie," Owens offered.

"You're very kind, Officer Owens," she said. "Did you enjoy your sandwich?"

"It was great, ma'am."

"I should have brought you something to drink," she said.

"That's okay."

"On the way out I'll ask one of the nurses to bring you some coffee," she said, then smiled and added, "I'll make it a cute one."

Owens blushed and said, "Thank you, ma'am."

She and Clint walked back up the hall to the lobby, where they stopped at the front desk and Annie made her request for coffee for the young policeman.

"I'll get someone to see to it," the nurse on duty said.

"See if you can send a cute nurse," Annie requested.

The nurse grinned and said, "He is rather a cute young man, isn't he?"

"Yes," Annie said, "he is."

She and Clint had started away from the desk when the nurse asked, "Did that other man find your husband's room?"

They stopped.

"What other man?" Clint asked.

"There was a man here asking about Mr. Butler," she said. "He claimed to be a friend of his."

"What did he want?" Clint asked, coming back to the desk.

"He asked what Mr. Butler's condition was."

"And you told him?"

"Y-yes."

"And what else?"

Warily, the nurse said, "That's, uh, all."

"Are you sure he didn't ask for the room number?"

"He, uh, may have—"

"Stay right here," Clint said to Annie, and ran back down the hall.

"What is it?" Officer Owens asked.

"Did a man come by here?"

"Just now? No."

"Okay," Clint said, "be alert, Owens. Someone was asking about Mr. Butler at the front desk."

"You can count on me, sir," Owens said, touching his sidearm confidently.

"Try not to fire that thing in the crowded halls, okay?"

"Don't worry."

Clint went back to where Annie was standing with the nurse.

"Did I do something awful?" the nurse asked.

"No," Annie said, patting her hand, "it was fine."

"Just don't give out any more information about Mr. Butler without checking with the doctor first, all right?"

"Yes, sir."

"Let's check outside, Annie."

They walked out the front door and stopped at the top of the steps. Clint checked the street but didn't see anyone suspicious.

"He was in the hospital, wasn't he?"

"Seems like it," Clint said. "Annie, the lieutenant asked me if you were carrying a gun. Are you?"

She hesitated, then said, "Yes," and showed him the two-shot derringer in her vest pocket.

"You should be ashamed," he said.

"I know, but—"

"That pocket can accommodate something bigger," he said. "Understand?"

She grinned and said, "Yes, sir."

TWENTY-THREE

When they got back to Annie's hotel again, Clint said, "Pack a bag."

"Why?"

"You're coming with me."

"To the Waldorf?"

"Yes."

"Clint," she said, "I'm a married woman—"

"I'll get you your own room."

"I can't let you pay for—"

"We'll let Cody pay for it."

"But I don't work for the Colonel—"

"We'll make it part of his package to woo you," Clint said. "Just pack a bag."

"Enough for overnight?"

"We'll come back and get the rest," he said. "When

Frank gets out, we'll put you both in the Waldorf, where I can keep an eye on you."

"Okay," she said. "You're the boss."

"And don't forget that bigger gun."

"I've got more guns," she said, "then clothes."

"Put it on Colonel Cody's bill," Clint told the clerk at the Waldorf.

"Uh, sir," the clerk said, "I can't do that."

"Get me your manager."

The clerk disappeared, and reappeared with an older man Clint had never seen before.

"Can I help you, Mr. Adams?"

"I want Miss Annie Oakley and Mr. Frank Butler to have a room here, and I want it on Colonel Cody's bill."

"Of course, sir," the manager said. "We have instructions from the Colonel to extend you every courtesy and give you anything you want."

"Anything?" Clint asked.

"Those are the Colonel's instructions."

"Then I would like Mr. and Mrs. Butler to have the honeymoon suite," Clint said.

"Clint!" Annie blushed.

"As you wish, sir," the manager said. He turned to the clerk and said, "The honeymoon suite."

"Yes, sir!"

"Mrs. Butler—Miss Oakley—please let me know if there is anything else I can do for you, and your husband when he arrives. My name is Stuart."

"You've already done quite enough, uh, Stuart."

"My pleasure, ma'am." He turned to Clint. "Sir."

"Thank you, Stuart."

Before he left, Stuart pulled the clerk aside—out of

earshot—and appeared to give him a stiff talking to. After that Clint and Annie had no further problems.

"Nice room," Clint said, "but you must have had rooms like this in Europe."

"Sometimes," she said.

"After all," Clint said, "you were playing to kings and queens and . . . czars?"

"And czarinas," she said, sitting on the huge canopy bed. "But I got so tired, Clint. I couldn't shoot straight I was so dizzy. And homesick. We had to come back." She rubbed both hands over her pretty face. "And we had to come back to this. Frank could have been killed today."

Clint walked over and sat next to her on the bed, putting his arm around her.

"Take it easy," he said. "If Wells had wanted Frank dead, he'd be dead."

"Then what does he want?"

"I don't know," Clint said, "but I'm going to try to find out."

Clint left Annie in her room to rest, and went back down to the front desk.

"What's your name?"

"Bennett, sir."

"I didn't mean to get you into trouble, Bennett," he said to the clerk, slipping him some money.

"That's all right, sir."

"Take it," Clint said. "Your boss said to keep me happy, right?"

The young man smiled, took the money and said, "Right."

"I'd like to leave a message for Colonel Cody."

"He just came in, sir," the clerk said. "Went up to his room."

"Good," Clint said. "Would you have someone go to his room and ask him to meet me in the bar?"

"Of course, sir," the clerk said. "My pleasure."

Clint gave him another dollar and said, "Thank you, Bennett."

He left the desk and walked across the lobby to the bar. It was time to bring Cody deeper into things, and maybe another name from his past visits to New York.

A man called Delvecchio.

TWENTY-FOUR

When Cody walked in, he was still in full regalia. All of the well-dressed men in the room watched him as he strutted across to Clint's table, where Clint was already waiting with two full mugs of beer.

"We should eat here," Cody said. "I'm starved."

"From the way I understand it," Clint said, "you can have anything you want."

"I can?"

"Well," Clint said, "apparently you've made those arrangements for me. I assume they extend to you, as well."

"Ah."

"Yes, ah. I've taken advantage of your generosity and arranged a room for Annie and Frank."

"Is she going to sign?"

"That doesn't matter," Clint said, and went on to tell Cody about Frank's attack.

"My God," Cody said, "are you sure he's all right?"

"He'll be getting out of the hospital tomorrow," Clint said. "I think you should pay his hospital bill."

"Me?" Cody asked. "Why should I do that?"

"Because you want Annie to sign."

"Oh, all right," Cody said.

"And you'll keep them here in the Waldorf until all this is settled?" Clint asked.

"Yes, yes," Cody said. "I'm generous to a fault, I know."

"That's what everybody says about you."

"Where did you have them put them?"

"The honeymoon suite."

"The honeymoon—That'll cost a fortune."

"And if Annie signs, you'll make a fortune."

"If Annie signs, and you sign, I'll make a fortune," Cody reminded him.

"I told you—"

"Don't say no yet," Cody said. "Well, I guess I know why the two of you didn't come out today. How about tomorrow?"

"That's why I wanted to see you," Clint said. "Annie and I will pick up Frank at the hospital and come out to see your operation."

"Good, good. Let's finish these beers and go into the restaurant for a proper meal," Cody said.

"Let me go upstairs and see if Annie's hungry."

"That's a fine idea," Cody said, standing up. "I'll meet both of you in there."

•   •   •

When Clint knocked on Annie's door, she answered it, bleary-eyed.

"I'm sorry," he said. "Were you asleep already?"

"No, not yet."

"Cody's here, and he and I were going to have dinner. I wanted to see if you were hungry."

"I am," she said, "but I'm more tired than hungry."

"All right," he said. "Why don't I come and get you for breakfast in the morning?"

"That sounds good," she said. "I'll be famished by then."

"Okay," he said. He took a moment to tell her that Cody would not only be paying for the room, but also for Butler's hospital bill.

"You got him to do that, didn't you?" she said. "I know he didn't offer."

"No, he didn't," Clint said, "but he readily agreed."

She came into his arms and gave him a hug with her head against his chest.

"You're such a good friend."

She was dressed for bed and he could feel the heat of her body against him, and the hardness of her small breasts. He was a good friend and he wanted to stay that way, so he eased her away from him and said, "I'll see you in the morning, then. Good night."

"Good night, Clint."

TWENTY-FIVE

"She's not coming?" Cody asked when Clint entered the dining room alone.

"She's too tired," Clint said, taking a seat.

"I ordered three steak dinners," Cody said. "We'll have to eat all three."

"I think we can manage."

The waiter came with the three meals and looked confused.

"Just put them down, son," Cody said. "We'll sort it out."

The waiter did as he was told, then went to get the three beers Cody had also ordered. By the time he returned with them, Clint and Cody had successfully turned the three steak dinners into two.

"Frank see who hit him?" Cody asked.

"No, but he heard him. He swears it's this Vernon Weeks, the man who's been following Annie."

"What the hell does he want?" Cody asked.

"I don't know," Clint said, "but I think I'm going to have to have somebody else baby-sit Annie while I try to find him."

"Who? Me? I'm not a baby-sitter."

"Not you," Clint said. "I know someone who lives here in New York—in Brooklyn, actually. He's a private detective."

"And you're gonna hire him?"

"No," Clint said, "you are."

"You're pushin' it, Clint," Cody said. "You're gonna have to start givin' me somethin', too."

"Like what?"

Cody thought a moment. "Three months with my show."

"A week."

"Two months."

"Two weeks."

"Six weeks."

"I guess you're trying to get me to four."

Cody slapped his hand down on the table. "Four it is! You go and hire your private detective. What's his name?"

"Delvecchio."

"That's it?"

"That's all I know," Clint said. "It's all I need to know. He helped me out last time I was here. He's a good man."

"Okay, then," Cody said. "What else?"

Clint sat back. "I'm not ready to trade more of my life," he said. "And just because I agree to four weeks doesn't mean Annie will."

"She will."

Now Clint sat forward. "Don't make her trade, Bill."

Cody matched looks with Clint for a few moments, then said, "Okay, I won't. She'll sign on her own, anyway."

They made a dent in their dinners—or dinner-and-a-half each—and then Cody asked, "Did you ever find out who that fella was who's been followin' *you*?"

Clint put his fork down. "No."

"You forgot about him, didn't you?"

"I sort of did."

Cody gestured with his fork. "Maybe he's out there now," he said. "You want us to go out and take a look?"

"After dinner, sure," Clint said. "You don't want something for the help?"

Cody spread his arms and asked, "What are friends for?"

"Sometimes," Clint said, "I wonder."

Clint and Cody walked across the lobby to check outside.

"The chief still with you?" Clint asked.

"Where else would Sitting Bull go?" Cody asked.

"You gonna use him to try to get Annie to sign?"

"Would I do that?" Cody asked. "The old man still thinks of her as his daughter. No, I won't do that, either."

When they reached the front door, Cody said, "Wait here. I know where a side exit is. Give me ten minutes to get into place, then step outside. If somebody's out there watching you, I'll see him."

"It's dark."

"Bog moon out tonight," Cody said. "Don't worry. I still got the eyes for it."

Clint didn't doubt that. He was about to say something

to that effect, but when he turned his head Cody was gone.

Still moved like an Indian Scout, too.

Clint waited exactly ten minutes, then stepped outside. He looked around but didn't see anything or anybody. Maybe the man had given up.

Clint stepped back inside and waited. Cody appeared in minutes.

"Nobody out there," he said. "Maybe he gave up."

"For the night, maybe," Clint said. "I'll check again in the morning."

"Come and get me for breakfast," Cody said. "I'll help you."

"I have to get Annie first, then you," Clint said. "See you in the morning, Bill."

TWENTY-SIX

Clint slept well that night. He could still smell Karyn Walker in the room, but the sheets had been changed on the bed. He was hoping she'd knock on his door that night, but she didn't, so he fell asleep and slept well.

In the morning the sun woke him. He went to the window and looked out. People walking back and forth on Park Avenue, cabs, buggies, a trolley. Nobody standing in a doorway across the street. Didn't mean somebody wasn't there, though.

He got up, got washed and dressed and went to Annie's room one floor up. She answered the door bright-eyed and wide awake.

"Where have you been?" she demanded. "I've been up for hours and I'm starving."

"Hours?"

"Well, maybe an hour."

"Cody's going to join us for breakfast," he said. "Is that all right?"

"I don't care who eats with us," Annie said, stepping out into the hall and closing the door to her room, "as long as I eat."

Clint patted her down and took a gun from her vest pocket. He smiled, took his Colt New Line from the small of his back. They were identical.

"We have the same taste," she said. "I like it because it's small and accurate."

He handed her gun back to her and put his own away.

"I like it because when I hit somebody with it," he said, "they go down."

Cody's room was actually down the hall from Annie's, as it was one of the larger rooms in the hotel. As they approached it, the door opened and he stepped out. His long, blond hair was gleaming, his mustache and beard impeccably trimmed, and he was dressed down, which meant his soft leather jacket did not have quite as much fringe as it usually did. He was still wearing a boiled white shirt, a bolo tie and sharply seamed trousers. His boots had enough silver on them to pay Clint's hotel bill, including both toes.

"Good mornin', you two," he said. "I was gettin' hungry waitin' for you."

"So was I," Annie said. "Mornin', Colonel."

When Cody got close enough, he gave Annie a hug.

"I'm sorry about Frank, Annie," he said. "How's he doin'?"

"I'm hopin' he stayed in the hospital overnight, like he was supposed to," Annie said. "If he did, then we'll be pickin' him up after breakfast."

"Good," Cody said. "I'll look forward to seein' him with the two of you out on Staten Island later today. I'm havin' some food brought in so we'll eat well."

"Thank you, Colonel."

The three of them went down to the restaurant and were seated without fanfare—but, of course, Cody attracted a lot of attention without any help.

They ordered breakfast, and as the waiter was pouring coffee, Cody asked Annie, "Did Clint tell you the news?"

Clint gave Cody a quick look.

"What? She wasn't supposed to know?"

"Know what?" Annie asked. "What's goin' on?"

"Clint has agreed to sign for a four-week run with me," Cody said.

She looked at Clint. "When did that happen?"

"Just last night," Clint said.

"Why?"

"The details aren't important."

Annie looked at Cody. "What did you make him trade for?"

"Me?" Cody asked.

"Annie—" Clint said.

"No," Annie said, "I want to know."

"Well," Cody said, "I'm payin' for you and Frank to stay here, I'm payin' Frank's hospital bill, and I'm payin' for a private detective Clint knows to protect you."

"A private detective?" Annie asked.

"Annie," Clint said, "I can't protect you and find Vernon Weeks, so I'm bringing in some help. A friend of mine."

"And Cody's payin'?"

"Indeed I am."

"And for that you get four weeks of Clint's life?"

"So far," Cody said, with a mischievous smile. "We dickered, and I don't think the dickering is done."

"That's not fair!" Annie said. "You're takin' advantage of Clint's helpin' me and Frank."

"Annie," Clint said, "it's all right."

"No, it's not," she said. "All right, Colonel, if you've got Clint for four weeks then you've got me for the same four weeks."

"Excellent!"

"Annie!"

"It's only fair," she insisted.

"Do you want to make that kind of decision without consulting Frank?" Clint asked.

"Frank will see it my way, Clint," she said. "Don't worry."

"Then it's done," Cody said. "I'll have the papers for the two of you to sign this afternoon."

"You don't waste any time, do you?" Clint asked.

"I'm sure he's had the papers ready for weeks," Annie said. "He was just waitin' to fill in the time."

"It's just good business to be prepared," Cody said.

At that point the waiter came with their breakfast and they broke off the discussion while they ate. Cody kept up a running conversation about other things, but he was mostly talking to himself.

After breakfast Cody left for Staten Island while Clint and Annie asked the doorman to get them a cab to take them to St. John's Hospital.

"Clint, I'm sorry this has cost you four weeks," Annie said.

"Cody usually gets his way, doesn't he?"

"Unfortunately, yes," she said, "but don't make any

more deals with him on our account, okay?"

"Not without discussing it with you and Frank first," Clint amended. "How's that?"

"Fine . . . I guess."

TWENTY-SEVEN

When they got to the hospital, Annie was very happy to find out that Butler had stayed put for the night.

"Never moved a muscle," Officer Owens told her when they reached the door.

"Were you here all night?" she asked.

"Yes, ma'am."

"But . . . why?"

"No one ever came to relieve me."

"That's my fault, Officer," Clint said. "I asked the lieutenant to put a man on the door—and asked for you, in fact—but I forgot to tell him to relieve you."

"No problem, sir."

"Officer," Annie said, "you go home and get some sleep, and thank you for all your help."

"It was my pleasure, ma'am." He looked at Clint. "If

you need any more help, you know where to find me."

"I do," Clint said. "Thanks."

When Owens left, Clint hoped the kid would make it home before he fell asleep.

As Annie and Clint entered the room together, they caught Frank Butler pulling on his trousers.

"It's about time you two showed up," he said. "I've had enough of this place."

"Can't say I blame you," Clint said. "I hate hospitals."

"Frank!" Annie snapped, as her husband started unwinding the turbanlike bandage from his head.

"I can't get my hat on!" Butler complained. "Besides, there's a smaller bandage underneath."

When he finished unwinding, they saw that he was telling the truth. There was a small bandage on his forehead, where the barrel or butt had bounced off.

He pulled on his boots, then stood up and put on his hat.

"I'm ready," he said. "Where are we going?"

"Back to the hotel first," Annie said, "to get our things."

"To get them and go where?"

"We'll tell you on the way."

When they left the room, Butler asked, "Do we have to stop and pay the bill?"

"It's being taken care of," Clint said, "by Cody."

"Cody?" Butler asked. "How did we work that out?"

"Clint did," Annie said, "and we'll tell you about that, too. Let's just go outside and get a cab."

By the time they got back to the hotel near Madison Square, Frank Butler had been filled in on everything.

"I hope you're not angry with me for agreeing to four

weeks, Frank," Annie said, as they stepped down from the cab.

"Of course not," Butler said.

"I told Clint you would back my decision."

"It's Cody I'm angry with," Butler said. "He's taking advantage of the situation."

"He's a businessman," Clint said. "That's his job."

"Well," Butler said, "at least he's paying for it. Getting the honeymoon suite at the Waldorf was a good move, Clint."

"You two go on upstairs and pack the rest of your things," Clint said. "I'm going to wait out here and look around."

"All right," Annie said. "It won't take long."

As Annie and Butler went into the hotel, Clint stood outside, eyeing the buildings across the street. Once he got ahold of Delvecchio and put him on Annie and Butler, he'd go across and check the buildings out, but right now he stared at the windows, wondering if anyone was staring back.

Across the street there were actually three men staring back.

"Get away from the window," Weeks said, "before he sees you."

The two men backed up along with him.

"How'd you know they'd come back here?" the first man asked.

"They had to collect their belongings in order to move into the Waldorf."

"So where do we go from here?"

"We leave now and head over to the Waldorf," Weeks said. "That'll be their next stop. After that, we each follow our own targets." He looked at the second man. "You got anything to say?"

"No," the man said. "I just do what I'm told—and what I'm paid to do."

Weeks looked at the first man and said, "You may have found yourself a good man here. I guess that will remain to be seen."

The second man just stared at Weeks, who grinned at him.

"You two get going," Weeks said. "I want to watch Adams some more."

"C'mon," the first man said to the second. "See ya, Weeks."

"Yeah."

The two men left and Weeks risked a peek out the window at Adams, who was still peering up at the building Weeks was in. Vernon Weeks wondered if maybe he shouldn't change targets.

TWENTY-EIGHT

Clint got Annie Oakley and Frank Butler properly ensconced in their Waldorf honeymoon suite, then agreed to meet them in two hours' time to go out to Staten Island to see Cody. He hoped that within that two hours he'd be able to arrange to contact the private detective Delvecchio. For that he needed help.

He went to the Waldorf lobby and found the desk clerk Bennett on duty.

"Good mornin', Mr. Adams," Bennett said as Clint approached the desk. "Can I do something for you?"

"Yes, Bennett," Clint said. "I need to get a message to a man in Brooklyn."

"A man?"

"A man named Delvecchio," Clint said. "A detective. Can you get me somebody who can do that?"

"Do you have an address?"

"I know where he lived a couple of years ago," Clint said. "I don't know if he's still there."

Bennett supplied a piece of paper and a pencil.

"Write down your message and I'll see that it's delivered, Mr. Adams."

Clint wrote his message and added everything he knew about Delvecchio's whereabouts.

"I have to go out to Staten Island today," Clint said. "How do I get there?"

"The ferry," Bennett said, "downtown. Just tell the cabdriver. By the time you return, I'll have word about your message."

"Good," Clint said. "Thanks." He took out some money and handed it to Bennett. "For you, and for the messenger."

"We both thank you."

"Will you be working tonight?"

"Probably not," Bennett said, "but I'll leave word for you."

"Good enough."

Clint had gotten that chore accomplished more quickly than he'd thought he would. It left him with some free time.

He turned back to Bennett and asked, "Where's the nearest exit without going out the front?"

He didn't know it, but he used the same exit Cody had used the night before. It left him on a side street, and he walked up to the corner of Park Avenue and then crossed over. Across the street were some businesses, some buildings that catered to offices, and another hotel. Anywhere in one of those buildings there could have been someone watching. Also any of the doorways. But the street corners, as far as he could see, were devoid of anyone watching the Waldorf's entrance.

He was tempted to simply walk down the street and have a good long look around, but that would be making an unnecessary target of himself. Instead, he picked out a doorway for himself and settled in to spend an hour just watching . . .

After the hour was up and nothing had been accomplished, Clint crossed the street back to the Waldorf side, retraced his steps to the side door and reentered the hotel. If someone was following him, or watching the hotel, Clint still hadn't spotted him . . . but the time would come soon enough.

When Clint got to the lobby, he was about to go into the bar, which had just opened, when he saw someone he knew come walking through the front door. He decided to just stand where he was and see if the person was there to see him.

TWENTY-NINE

"Adams," Lieutenant Egan said.

"Lieutenant, what a nice surprise."

Egan looked around the lobby. "Ain't much call for me to be here," he said. "Why don't you take me into the bar and buy me a drink?"

"Sure," Clint said, "why not?"

He led the way into the bar, bought two beers and took Egan to a table. Since the bar had just opened, they were the only two men there. Egan looked around at the crystal and leather, and breathed it all in.

"This is a nice way to drink," he said, lifting the glass to his mouth. "And that's good beer."

"To what do I owe this pleasure, Lieutenant?" Clint asked.

"I'm curious about you, Adams."

"In what way?"

"What is it about you that attracts the Roosevelts, and the Barnums, and the Buffalo Bill Codys?"

"My charm."

"Ah," Egan said, "well, charm is somethin' I wouldn't know anything about."

"I don't know," Clint said. "Everybody's got their own brand of charm."

"Not me," Egan said. "I've got none, and I know it. But you know what I do have?"

"What's that?"

"A nose."

One big as a potato, Clint thought, but he kept that comment to himself.

"Everybody's got one of those, Lieutenant."

"Not like mine, though. Mine's special."

"What makes it so special?"

"The things I can do with it."

"Like what?"

"Well, for one thing," Egan said, "I can smell trouble brewing from a mile away."

"And you smell it now?"

"Even before I saw you at the hospital yesterday," the policeman said, "but much more since. So I figured I'd track you down and see what you had to say for yourself."

Clint shrugged and said, "I'm here visiting friends, Lieutenant."

"Ah, there's somethin' else my nose is good for."

"And what's that?"

Egan tapped it and said, "I can tell when somebody's not tellin' me the truth."

"I'm not lying."

"Lies, that's somethin' else," Egan said. "I can smell

lies, and you ain't lyin'—but you ain't tellin' me the truth, either."

"That is a talented nose, Lieutenant," Clint commented.

"Yeah, it is," Egan said. "I get a lot of use out of it."

Clint checked the time on the elegant, expensive clock that stood up against the wall next to the bar.

"Got someplace to go?" Egan asked. "Am I keepin' you?"

"I've got about fifteen minutes," Clint said, "and then I'm supposed to have lunch with some friends of mine out on Staten Island."

"Out at Cody's show?"

"That's right."

"You got any idea when that's supposed to open?" Egan said. "I been wantin' to see that."

"Gonna take the wife and the little ones?" Clint asked.

"No wife," Egan said, "no little ones. Just me. I hear it's a helluva show."

"I don't think you'll be disappointed."

"Annie Oakley in it?"

"That's what I hear."

"And Sitting Bull, right?"

"Yep."

"That old chief ... he must be pretty old by now, wouldn't you say?"

"Oh, I would."

"And what about you?"

"What about me?"

"You gonna be in the show?"

"I might."

Egan looked surprised.

"You gonna be shootin' against Miss Oakley? Oh, 'scuse me, Mrs. Butler."

"That's what I understand Cody has in mind."

"Well, I'll be—that would be somethin' to see, now wouldn't it?"

"I guess so."

"How did Colonel Cody swing that, I wonder."

"Charm," Clint said.

"Well," Egan said, lifting his beer mug, "here's to charm."

THIRTY

When Clint, Annie and Butler stepped off the ferry, a man approached them, removing his hat.

"Would you folks be Miss Annie Oakley and company?" he asked.

"That's right," Clint said, before Annie could protest. "She's Annie Oakley, and we're company."

"Colonel Cody sent me to fetch you."

"He did?" Butler asked. "How did he know which ferry we'd be on?"

The man shrugged and said, "He 'ssumed."

"Let's not look a gift horse in the mouth, Frank," Clint said. "We need a ride out to the site."

"What's your name?" Annie asked the man. "I haven't seen you with Colonel Cody before."

"My name is Styles, ma'am," the man said. "He jes' hired me to drive around folks like you."

"Well, okay, Styles," Clint said. "Drive us around."

It was not a long ride, but it was a ride through a whole lot of nothing until they got to the point where they could see all the tents.

"Doesn't look as big as the European show," Butler commented.

"He's only doin' this to try out some new acts, Frank," Annie said. "At least, that's what he told me at dinner the other night."

"So he wants you and Clint to bring in some big money, plus he's keepin' his overhead low," Butler said. "Like Clint said, he's a good businessman."

Styles drove them right up to one of the big tents, and Clint could see that tables of food had been set out for them. He wondered if the same setup had been there yesterday. If it had, he hoped that when they didn't arrive, Cody had at least let the crew eat it all.

As they were stepping down from the buggy, Cody came walking over with his arms spread wide. He had changed into one of his fringe jackets. The sun reflected off all the silver that was on his boots.

"You made it this time," Cody said. "Frank, I'm happy to see you up and around."

Butler shook hands with Cody. "Thanks, Colonel," he said. "I'm happy to *be* up and around."

Cody hugged Annie and shook hands with Clint.

"Well, this is it, children," Cody said. "This is the lay-out, home to you and Annie for four weeks, Clint. I hope Annie cleared that with you, Frank."

"She explained it to me, Colonel," Butler said. "We're

grateful to you for handling the hospital bill, and upgrading our accommodations."

"Happy to do it, Frank," Cody said. "I hope you don't take it personal about me not signin' you."

"Sure I do, Colonel," Frank Butler said, "but what can I do about it?"

Cody stared at Butler for a moment, then laughed and said, "That's one of the things I really like about you, Frank. Your sense of humor. Come on, I got a bunch of food brought out here from the city. Let's chow down and then I'll show you around."

Lunch was impressive and Clint ate his fill. He didn't know how Cody had managed it, but he had cold beer out there, as well. Annie and Frank enjoyed it, too. It was just the four of them under that tent eating, though, and there was plenty of food left over when they were done.

"What happens to the leftovers, Colonel?" Annie asked. She got the question in before Clint could.

"You want me to let the crew eat it, don't you?" the showman asked.

"I think it would be nice."

"All right, then," Cody said. "I'll have Styles pass the word that there's food to be had, courtesy of Annie Oakley."

Annie was about to protest but Clint put his hand on her arm and said, "That'll be great, Colonel."

"Come on, then," Cody said. "I'll show you folks around."

There was nothing there that Annie Oakley and Frank Butler hadn't seen many times before. As for Clint, he had been to Cody's show a time or two and even to him this layout looked somewhat smaller than most.

Cody introduced Clint to some members of the show

he didn't know, but stopped for a longer introduction when they encountered a dark-haired woman in a tight cotton dress who was sitting at a table sewing what appeared to be some costumes.

"This is Mae Sinclair," Cody said. "Mae, meet Clint Adams, Annie Oakley and Frank Butler. Mae just joined us here during our New York stay."

Mae put aside her sewing and stood up. She was tall, and while not as full bodied as Karyn Walker had been, she still filled out her dress in impressive fashion.

"I'm very pleased to meet three such distinguished people," she said. She had a deep, husky, sultry voice that made chills run down Clint's spine. A quick look at Frank Butler revealed that he was feeling it, too. Clint hoped that Annie Oakley would not take this moment to glance over at her husband.

"Miss Sinclair," Clint said, shaking her hand.

"Please," she said, "call me Mae."

"Mae," Annie said, shaking the woman's hand. "Happy to meet you."

Clint heard something in Annie's tone he didn't like. Apparently, Mae's sultry voice had just the opposite effect on women that it had on men. It made them hate her. Annie hadn't even needed to look over at Butler.

"Miss Sinclair," Butler said, playing the situation just exactly right.

"Mae," Cody said, "I'd like to talk to Annie and Frank without Clint. Why don't you walk him around and show him a bit more of the operation?"

"It would be my pleasure, Colonel," Mae said, slipping her arm into Clint's. "That is, if Mr. Adams doesn't mind?"

"I don't mind at all, Mae," Clint said, "and please call me Clint."

THIRTY-ONE

"So what is it you do around here, Mae?" Clint asked as they walked away from the other three.

"I do a little of everything," she said, "or I will once the show starts. Believe it or not one of my roles will be as an Indian maiden."

"A beautiful Indian maiden, no doubt," Clint said.

"Why, thank you, sir." She hugged Clint's arm, bringing it right into contact with her full left breast.

Mae Sinclair appeared to be in her thirties, and was very tall for a woman, which helped her to carry her impressive bosom and hips. She'd make for a very full-bodied and interesting Indian maiden.

"How does Sitting Bull feel about you being an Indian?" Clint asked.

"Oh, he's an old softie," she said. "He doesn't mind at

all. In fact, he likes me—though not as much as he does Annie."

"Is he around today?" Clint asked. "I'm sure Annie would love to see him."

"He's always around," she said. "He lives out here, while most of us have rooms in Manhattan or Brooklyn."

"You can get to Brooklyn from here?" he asked.

"Oh yes," she said. "There's a ferry that goes there, too. Do you like Brooklyn?"

"I know someone who lives there."

"A lady friend, perhaps?"

"Just a friend."

"No lady friends in New York, Clint?"

"I have lots of friends, Mae," Clint said, "and some of them are ladies."

"Ooh, I can see I'm going to have to be careful of you," she said. "You have a way with words."

"Tell me what you were doing before you signed on with Colonel Cody," Clint said.

"Believe it or not, I was an actress."

"Now, why wouldn't I believe that?"

"Well," she said, "some people who have seen me act don't believe it. It wasn't something I did very well, so when Colonel Cody offered me a job, I took it."

"Where did the two of you meet?"

"The Colonel came to the theater one night," she said. "Apparently he was one of the people who didn't think I was much of an actress."

"I hope Cody wasn't that blunt."

"He was a perfect gentleman," she said. "Someone brought him backstage and he offered me a job. He said there was always room in his show for a beautiful woman."

"There's always room everywhere for a beautiful woman," Clint said.

"You're kind," she said. "I don't think Miss Annie Oakley felt that way a little while ago. I felt a definite chill from her when we shook hands."

"I'll bet you get that from a lot of women."

"I do," she said. "Why is that?"

"You don't know?"

"Because their men like me, I suppose," she said. "Men tend to like me, and I like them. I guess that's threatening to some women, isn't it?"

"Yes, it is."

"But . . . she and Frank are married."

"I'm afraid you have the same effect on married men you have on unattached ones, Mae."

"Really?" she asked. "Do I have that effect on you?"

"Definitely."

"Then I suppose you wouldn't mind if I did . . . this!"

THIRTY-TWO

Mae pulled Clint into an empty tent with strength that was not surprising, given her size. When she got him inside, she immediately molded herself to him and kissed him. Her mouth was hot and avid, and her hands were busy on him as well.

"I take it you don't mind?" she asked. Her mouth was still against his, her breath hot, and her hands had ahold of his crotch—an area that was making it very clear that he didn't mind. "I'm a little forward when I see something I want."

"Then I hope you won't mind if I return the favor?" Clint asked her.

"Oh," she said, breathily, "please do."

He slid his hands beneath her cotton dress and found himself holding her naked butt in his hands.

"I hate underwear," she said, again against his mouth.

"That," he said, kneading her ass while she pressed her crotch against his, "is very obvious."

"So is this," she said, sliding herself up and down his hardness.

They kissed again, and he slid one hand around to the front, still under her dress. He probed with his fingers, found her wet and slid his finger along her slit. She jumped as if she had been struck by lightning and lifted one leg up to open herself up to him. He hooked the leg on his arm so she could lean on him, and continued to finger her until she was soaking his hand.

"God!" she said, breaking away from a hot kiss. "You came along at just the right time. I want this so bad!"

Together they removed his gun belt, his trousers and underwear, and with all of that gathered down around his ankles—with his boots still on and her leg still hooked on his arm—he entered her in one swift move.

"Yessssss!" she hissed into his ear as he pierced her to the hilt.

He slid his other arm around so she could hook her other leg, and then, with him holding her like that, they began to fuck quickly, anxiously, rutting like animals. Clint was mindful of two things—that she was heavy and that at any moment they could be discovered. But the wetter she got, and the hotter she got, and the sharper her rutting odor became, the more he simply forgot about those things and applied himself to the task at hand.

He pulled her dress down off her shoulders, exposing her full breasts, which had nipples as dark as pennies. He kissed her skin, sucked her nipples and bit her as he continued to drive himself in and out of this woman he'd met maybe ten minutes ago.

They were leaning their combined weight against a tent pole, which dug into Clint's back. Still, he didn't even feel that as Mae became eager for her release. She braced herself with her hands on his shoulders and started saying, "Yes, yes, yes . . . y-yesssss . . ." as her time grew nearer.

Clint was ready to go off like Chinese fireworks, but he waited as long as he could. There was nothing romantic about this coupling. He wondered who would be in this empty tent with her now if he hadn't come along, but he counted himself lucky that he had.

"Oooh, God," she said, straining against him, beating on him with her fists, "come on, come on, come on . . ."

He wasn't sure if she was talking to herself or to him, but her words had an effect. He released the iron hold he had on himself and suddenly went off, spurting inside of her, his legs growing fatigued as he did. Mae's eyes went wide, and suddenly she was bucking on him even harder, her head thrown back, the cords on her neck standing out as she followed him over the edge, experiencing her own fireworks, inside her head, behind her tightly closed eyes and down further . . .

Clint knew that if they had been in a hotel room they would have tumbled onto a bed together. Now, however, he had to be careful not to fall over, or drop her. She reached behind him to grab onto the tent pole and try to help him. He set her legs down as gently as he could and slid out of her, still amazingly, even impressively hard.

"Oh God," she said, backing away from him, "look at you . . ."

"Mae . . . ," he said warningly, but the warning never came. Mae dropped down onto her knees and immediately engulfed his penis in her hot mouth. As she began to suck him, gripping his naked thighs, digging her nails into him, he grew even harder and once again was lost in the sensations of being with this unbelievably sexual creature. Her hair had tumbled down around her shoulders and breasts, and he was pressing back against the pole until he thought the tent would come down around them, and wouldn't that have been embarrassing?

But the tent didn't fall, the pole held, and his pole—buried in her mouth to the root—began to pulsate and then explode. She gripped his buttocks so he couldn't get away, and proceeded to suck him dry. He had to reach down and push her off him before it became painful.

"Stop!" he gasped. "Jesus, you're going to turn me inside out."

She ended up sitting on her butt in the dirt, staring up at him wide-eyed, sort of dazed.

Suddenly, she said, "Oh God, somebody could come here at any time."

"I know."

Hurriedly he pulled on his pants and strapped on his gun while she stood, brushed dirt off herself and rearranged her dress. They stood there for a moment, staring at each other, catching their breath, and then suddenly they started to laugh.

"I'm so sorry," she said, covering her mouth with her hands. "I don't know what came over me. Well, yes I do, but usually I can control myself when I get like that. I mean . . . I never grab the first man I see but . . . but there was something about you as soon as I met you . . . I knew I had to have you inside me . . ."

That made Clint feel a bit better about the encounter—that, apparently, it wasn't that she would have done this with just anybody. He remembered the chill he felt in his spine when he first heard her speak, and obviously there had been a connection there for both of them . . .

"We'd better find the Colonel and your friends before they start looking for us," she said.

"I guess we better."

"You don't think I'm just terrible, do you?"

"Mae," he said, as they exited the tent, "I think you were just wonderful!"

THIRTY-THREE

"Well," Cody said, when Clint and Mae came walking up to him, Annie and Butler, "where did you two get off to?"

"I was just showing Clint around and we got to talking and lost track of the time," Mae said. She'd straightened her hair as best she could, and her dress, but she still looked pretty disheveled to Clint. He had no idea how he looked, but Annie was giving them both a funny look, and he knew that she knew . . .

"I was just showing Annie the main tent where you and she could be performing," Cody said. "We've got all kinds of targets, even a mechanical trap machine."

"Sounds interesting," Clint said.

"And we're going to do posters with both your like-nesses on them. I mean, one of each of you, and then one together. I've got an artist who will capture you perfectly."

"It all sounds great," Frank Butler said. Clint knew he was joining in for Annie's sake, but was probably dying inside because he wasn't included.

"Well," Mae said, "I have to get back to work. It was nice meeting you all. Perhaps we can get together for dinner in Manhattan one night?"

"Well . . . ," Annie said.

"I don't know . . . ," Butler said.

"Capital idea!" Cody said. "Why don't I set that up for us?"

"As you wish, Colonel," Mae said. "You're the boss."

For a moment Clint wondered about Cody and Mae . . . but no, he knew when he'd been with a woman who hadn't had sex for a while. Unless, of course, Mae was simply always that eager.

She walked off, with Clint, Cody and Butler watching her butt twitch—Clint the only one who knew there was no underwear under there—and with Annie giving her dirty looks the whole way.

"She seems . . . nice," Annie said.

"Mae?" Cody said. "Mae's great. She was tryin' to be an actress when I met her, and I gave her a job right away."

"She told me she's going to be an Indian maiden," Clint said.

"Among other things," Cody said. "Speaking of Indians, the old chief would like to see you while you're here, Annie."

Now Annie's eyes lit up and she said, "Oh, I'd love to see him."

"Want to meet Sitting Bull, Clint?" Cody asked.

"The chief and I have met," Clint said, "once or twice, but that was a long time ago. I don't know if he'd remember."

"He's got an amazing memory," Cody said. "I'll bet he does. Well, come on, then, we'll all go and see him. I tried to put the old codger in a hotel, but he prefers staying out here in a tent . . ."

Cody walked them around behind the entire setup, to a field where a single tent stood. It was much larger than the tepees Sitting Bull had inhabited in his younger days.

"He likes his privacy," Cody said, "but I know he'll be glad to see you, Annie."

"Maybe Annie should go in first?" Butler suggested.

"Why not?" Cody said. "Come on, Annie, I'll take you in."

Annie nodded and followed Buffalo Bill Cody into Sitting Bull's tent.

"Well," Butler said, "how was it?"

"How was what?"

"You and Mae Sinclair."

"Was it that obvious?"

"Oh, yeah," Butler said, "to me, and probably to Annie. I don't know about the Colonel."

"I tell you, Frank," Clint said, "it was one of the most amazing experiences—"

He was cut off when Cody stuck his head out of the tent and said, "The chief would like you both to come in."

"Sure," Clint said, and then to Butler in a lower voice, "Later."

THIRTY-FOUR

"It is good to see you, daughter," Sitting Bull was saying to Annie as Clint and Butler entered with Cody.

"And you," Annie said. "I've missed you, you old coot."

Sitting Bull's face was deeply lined from the trials he'd lived through, and from his advanced years.

"Chief," Cody said, "you remember Frank Butler."

"Yes," Sitting Bull said, "my daughter's husband. You have treated her well. She looks happy."

"She looks rested, sir," Butler said. "She was worn out the last time you saw her."

Clint looked around the tent. It was spartan, with blankets tossed here and there and little else. Sitting Bull had apparently not become soft from traveling with Cody's show. Clint wondered if the old chief ever stayed in hotels. How must he have liked Europe? Clint wondered.

He was impressed by Sitting Bull's physical presence. His massive head sat upon broad shoulders, and while he only stood five foot eight he seemed larger than life. Here, after all, was the conqueror of Custer, the victor at the Little Big Horn. Here was the greatest Sioux chief of them all.

"And this is Clint Adams," Cody said.

"It is an honor to see the great chief of the Hunkpapa Sioux again. I don't know if you remember me—"

"Sitting Bull remember The Gunsmith," the older man said. "It would be difficult to forget one so accomplished. It is my honor to receive you."

"The honor is mine, Chief."

"Why don't we just say that you're both honored and leave it at that?" Cody asked.

"Daughter," Sitting Bull said, "we have much to catch up on."

"Annie has some papers to sign, Chief," Cody said.

The old man's eyes widened. "You are returning?"

"Only for a short time," she said.

"She and Clint are going to be with us for four weeks—at least four weeks."

"The Gunsmith will perform in Cody's show?"

"If it's good enough for the Sioux chief, it's good enough for me," Clint said.

"Colonel," Annie said, "I'm gonna stay and talk with the chief for a while."

"All right," Cody agreed. "Clint and Frank can look the papers over and you can sign when you come out."

Clint and Frank said goodbye to Sitting Bull, who by this time had his huge head pressed close to Annie's much smaller one. They were already deep in conversation by the time the other three men left the tent.

"It's amazing to think that's actually Sitting Bull," Clint said when they got outside.

"It's him, all right," Cody said. "I've got it documented."

"You don't have to convince me," Clint said. "I recognized him."

"Where are the papers you want Annie to sign, Colonel?" Butler asked. "I might as well give them a good going over."

"Everything is on the up and up, Frank."

"I'm sure it is, sir," Butler said, "but you know me. I read even the finest of print."

"I know, indeed," Cody said. "All right, let's go to my tent and you can both read them."

They followed Cody to a tent the same size as Sitting Bull's, but that's where the similarity ended. Inside was a table, a cot, a desk, even a chest of drawers. The paperwork was on top of the desk. Cody retrieved it and put two sets on the table where Clint and Frank could both sit and read.

"You fellas want some coffee while you do your readin'?" Cody asked.

"I'll have some," Butler said.

"Me, too."

"I'll go and fetch it."

As Cody left, Butler said, "I don't really want any, but I like the idea of Cody going to fetch it for us."

"So do I," Clint said. "Listen, I need a favor from you."

"Name it."

Clint looked down at the papers and gestured helplessly with his hands. "I really don't know much about these performance contracts . . ."

"You want me to check them over for you?"

"Please."

"No problem," Butler said. "I'll do the same thing for you I do for Annie."

"What's that?"

"Make sure Cody doesn't take too much of her."

"I appreciate it."

"And you have to do something for me."

"Name it."

Butler leaned in. "Tell me everything that happened with Mae Sinclair!"

THIRTY-FIVE

When Cody returned with the coffee, Clint pretended to be reading the contracts. Butler had already told him that he would be making some changes for both him and Annie, but that he wasn't going to let Cody know he'd finished reading them yet.

"I'm gonna wait for Annie to get here and then tell Cody we have to talk," he'd said.

"You just want to make him wait?"

"Exactly."

"I don't have a problem with that."

When Cody arrived, he was carrying a tray with a pot of coffee and four cups.

"I thought Annie might like some when she got here," he said, "and I'll join you. Still reading, I see?"

"I have a problem with some of the wording," Butler

said, "but I think it can be worked out. I'll just have to discuss it with Annie."

"No problem," Cody said. "What about you, Clint?"

"Oh, uh, same thing," Clint said, "a problem or two, nothing real big."

"Same problems, hmm?" Cody asked, eyeing them both suspiciously. "Why do I have the feeling I'm being double-teamed here?"

"Hey," Butler said, "the contracts should be the same, that's all. Also . . . can I see yours for a minute, Clint?"

Of course, he'd already looked over both contracts, but he was putting on a show for Cody.

"There's a little discrepancy in the money, Colonel."

"Well," Cody said, "Clint is a man, and he's The Gunsmith—"

"I don't have a problem with Annie getting the same money," Clint said.

"Mmm, I see," Cody said. "Well, if that's the way you want it—"

"And then there's the question of billing," Butler said.

"Well," Cody said, "Clint is the bigger draw here, Frank. He's the one with the big reputation—"

"Not in this arena he isn't," Butler said. "When it comes to sharpshooting, Annie's the draw. I'm sorry, Clint, but that's how I see it."

"You don't have to convince me, Frank," Clint said. "I have no problem being billed beneath Annie Oakley—"

"Now, just a doggone minute," Cody said. "I have a problem with it. You're a goddamn legend of the West, for pity's sake. You can't take second billing to a . . . a . . ."

"A what, Colonel?" Annie asked, entering the tent. "A girl?"

All the men turned their attention to her.

"Look," Clint said, "I have no problem with equal billing. Do you, Annie?"

"None whatsoever," Annie said. "Do we, Frank?"

"Well . . ."

"Frank?"

"No, we don't."

"Bill?" Clint asked.

"Fine," Cody said, throwing his hands in the air. "You want equal billing, you got it."

"Okay, then," Butler said, "make the changes, Colonel, and then we'll sign them."

"Nate usually handles that," Cody said. "I'll have to take the papers to him—why don't we have dinner at the Waldorf tonight and we can sign the papers then?" Suddenly, he was not nearly as annoyed as he'd seemed to be a few moments earlier.

"Dinner's fine with me," Clint said.

"Us, too," Butler said, and Annie nodded.

"Fine," Cody said. "Did you have a good visit with the chief, Annie?"

"Wonderful," she said. "I love that old man."

"Perfect," Cody said. "I'll have Styles take you all back to the ferry, then."

They all left the tent and walked back to where the buggy was waiting.

"Where did he get to?" Cody said, looking around. "I told him to stay available."

"Check the food," Clint said.

"Good idea. I'll be right back."

After Cody left, Annie folded her arms and asked, "Did you two gang up on him?"

"We might have," Clint said. "I asked Frank to read my contract as well as yours."

"Clint, you really don't mind sharing billing with me? After all, you are The Gunsmith."

"It's not a problem with me, Annie," Clint said. "Talk to your husband."

"Oh, I don't have a problem if Annie doesn't," Frank said. "I was just trying to give Cody a hard time."

"I get the feeling Cody got just what he wanted," Clint said.

"There's something I want," Annie said.

"What's that?" Clint asked.

"I want to know what went on between you and that dark-haired hussy Mae Sinclair!"

THIRTY-SIX

As they reentered the Waldorf sometime later, having been left off right in front by Styles, Annie asked, "Were we followed at all today?"

"I didn't see anyone," Clint said. "Not going to the ferry, or returning."

"Maybe he gave up," Butler said.

"I wish he would," Annie said, "but somehow I doubt it."

"I agree with Annie," Clint said. "I don't think he'd attack you and then leave the city. Something is up, and I'm going to find out what it is."

"What about protecting Annie?" Butler said.

"I've got that covered, Frank," Clint said, looking past both of them at the man who was approaching them.

"Annie Oakley and Frank Butler," Clint said, "meet Delvecchio."

They both turned to look at the smiling young man.

"Just Delvecchio?" Annie asked.

"That's all he wants to be known by," Clint said. "Maybe you can charm his first name out of him while he's protecting you."

"You're a bodyguard and a detective?" Frank Butler asked, shaking hands with Delvecchio.

"I can cook, too," Delvecchio said. "How are you, Clint? It's good to see you."

"You, too." They shook hands.

"I was surprised to get your message," the detective said, "but not surprised that it said come to the Waldorf. You stayed here last time, too."

"Well," Clint said, "this time somebody else is footing the bill—Buffalo Bill Cody."

"Ah," Delvecchio said, "well, that shouldn't surprise me, either. A couple of legends of the Old West like you would know each other, wouldn't you?"

"Not only that," Clint said, "but I'll be working for him for four weeks when his show opens."

"How did that happen?"

"I'll tell you later," Clint said. "Why don't the three of you go to the honeymoon suite and get acquainted."

"Honeymoon suite?"

"We'll tell you how that happened," Annie said.

Speaking to Delvecchio, Clint said, "Work out your routine with them, Del. Basically you're protecting Annie, but Frank had a bit of a, uh, mishap that landed him in the hospital. They'll tell you all about it."

"Okay," Delvecchio said. "I'll be right with the two of you. I just need to talk to Clint about something."

"We'll wait by the stairs," Butler said.

As they walked away, Delvecchio asked, "What's the relationship here?"

"What do you mean?"

"I mean, you and Annie, at any time . . ."

"No, no, nothing like that," Clint said. "Frank and I are old friends. I just met Annie during this trip to New York. Frank asked me to come and help them."

"A couple of sharpshooters like them need help?" Delvecchio asked.

"They're show people, Delvecchio," Clint said. "I doubt either of them has ever fired a shot at another person."

"Oh, I get it."

"Just keep them safe until I find out who's after them," Clint said. "Well, actually we know who it is."

"Who?"

"A man named Vernon Weeks."

"Weeks?"

"Do you know him?"

"Not Vernon," Delvecchio said, "but the name Weeks strikes a chord with me."

"Well, think it over and let me know what you come up with," Clint said.

"You need some help getting around the city, you let me know," Delvecchio said. "I can get you another man."

"I'll keep it in mind."

"Okay," Delvecchio said, "let me get to my people— oh, one more thing."

"What's that?"

"Who's paying me?"

"Cody."

"So we're both on his payroll?"

"Looks that way."

Delvecchio smiled. "I'll adjust my fees accordingly."

"I thought you might."

Delvecchio slapped Clint on the back and said, "Really good to see you, Clint. Before you leave New York, we'll have to sit down over a few and catch up."

"I'm all for that," Clint said. "All the more reason to get this wrapped up as quickly as possible."

"I hear you."

Delvecchio made his way across the lobby, and he, Annie and Butler started up the stairs.

Now that he was free of worrying about Annie, all Clint needed was a place to start.

THIRTY-SEVEN

Vernon Weeks looked up as the two men entered the Bowery bar he'd asked them to meet him at.

"What a dump," the first man said. "You really drink here?"

"It's an out-of-the-way place for us to meet," Weeks said. "Get yourself some beer."

The first man looked at the second, who went to the bar to fetch the beer.

"What's goin' on?" the first man asked Weeks. "We were gettin' ready to make our move."

"There's a slight complication."

"What kind of complication?"

"Adams has brought in some help."

"So?"

"A detective named Delvecchio."

"I don't know him."

The second man came over with the two beers and sat down at the table with them.

"You know a detective named Delvecchio?" the first man asked him.

"Sure," the man replied. "Brooklyn, right?"

"That's right," Weeks said. "He's from Brooklyn."

"He's in this?"

"He is."

"He's no pushover."

"What's his part gonna be?" the first man asked.

"I think Adams is going to put him on Annie Oakley," Weeks said.

"Why would he do that?"

"So he's free to look for me."

"Well," the first man said, "he won't be lookin' for you if he's dead."

"And you're ready to move?"

"Today," the first man said.

"All right," Weeks said. "If Adams is paying Delvecchio, and Adams gets killed, what will the detective do?" He was directing the question to the second man.

"This Delvecchio works for money," the second man said. "If the man who's supposed to be paying him gets killed, he'll walk away."

"You sure?" Weeks asked.

"Positive."

"What makes you so positive?" the first man asked.

"Delvecchio worked with my cousin for a while."

"Does he know you on sight?" Weeks asked.

"He never met me."

"Never even saw you?"

"Not once."

"Okay, then," Weeks said. "If you two take care of Adams today, this will all get a lot easier for me."

"Consider it done," the first man said.

"Okay," Weeks said. "Go do it."

"I didn't even drink my beer," the first man said.

"You talk too much," Weeks said. "You can have a beer after the job is done."

While he was talking, the second man made sure he got his beer by chugging the whole thing down. He set the mug on the table with a bang.

"I'm ready."

"Get it done, then."

The first man scowled, looked at his untouched beer, then said to the second man, "Aw, come on."

THIRTY-EIGHT

Clint found that the building right across the street from Annie and Butler's old hotel was abandoned. He couldn't find a way in from the front, so he went around back. He found a door that had been boarded up, but the board had been loosened. He was able to slip inside without much trouble.

It was dark but he was in a stairwell. As he went up the stairs, it got lighter. There were four floors, and each floor had windows facing the street. Clint took the time to check all of them.

When he got to the third floor, he found what he was looking for. There were boot prints in the dusty floor, and discarded cigarettes, most of them smoked only halfway down. He prowled the room a bit more, trying to read signs on the floor, but this wasn't the West, where the ground and the flora and fauna revealed a lot about a man you were tracking, This was the city, and the hardwood floor revealed little beyond the boot prints. Since that was all he had to work with—that and the cigarette butts— Clint studied the prints so he'd be able to recognize them if he saw them again.

He looked out the window and saw that any experienced marksman would have a very clear shot at anyone coming out the front door of the hotel. If Vernon Weeks had wanted either Annie Oakley or Frank Butler dead, he could have accomplished it very easily. Obviously, killing one or the other was not his ultimate goal.

So what was?

The first shot missed by a foot, but only because he tripped while trying to slide out the way he'd slid in. His foot slipped and he stumbled coming out the back door. The bullet struck the loosened board a foot above his head—where his chest would have been.

Instead of regaining his balance, he immediately recognized the sound of the shot and the slap of the bullet into the wood and went with the stumble, taking himself to the ground as the second shot sounded.

He rolled, drew his gun and came up on one knee. The shots had not been fired from a distance, because they were fired with pistols, not with rifles—and yes, only two shots was enough for his educated ear to realize that there were two shooters.

He was in an area between two rows of buildings, and the shots had to have come from the row opposite the building he'd just come out of. He needed one more shot to be fired in order to locate them—but he also needed that shot to miss. However, he also needed to be looking—not ducking—when the shot was fired, so he did what he hoped neither of the shooters would expect of him.

He got up and started running—hopefully, right at them.

"What the hell is he doing?" the first man asked. "He's coming right at us."

The second man knew what Clint was doing—he was being smart. Who in his right mind would run right into the teeth of the bullets?

"Don't fire again—" the second man started to say, but it was too late. The first man fired a shot, then a second, effectively giving away their position.

"Damn it, why aren't you firing?" the first man asked. Each of his shots had missed.

"Because that's what he wanted," the second man said. "Now he knows where we are."

"Well . . . ," the first man said, and when he could not think of a defense for himself, he added, ". . . let's get out of here, then!"

Clint saw the two muzzle flashes, heard the bullets slap into the ground around him. Obviously, he'd accomplished just what he'd hoped to. He'd rattled at least one shooter into firing and missing, and he'd located them. The building they were in was right across from him, and the window was on the second floor.

Now he had to decide whether to try to find a way in from the back, or run around to the front, figuring that they'd missed so they'd be running. He decided on the latter.

As he reached the building without any more shots being fired, he knew he'd guessed right—they were on the run. He found an alley that would bring him through to the street in front, and as he got there he saw two men running down the street, toward Madison Square.

He took off after them.

The two gunmen hit the street running just as Clint came out of the alley.

"He's behind us!" the second man said.

"Run!" the first man said, and in that one word the second man heard panic.

He was only working for the first man—whom he considered clearly inferior to himself—because of the money, but now that man was going to get himself killed. The second man was determined not to let the man also get him killed.

"Split up!" he shouted.

"Wha—" the first man stammered. He turned, saw his "employee" veer off, and hesitated for just a moment.

A deadly, fatal moment.

It was late in the day and the street was crowded with people heading home from work. The shooters weaved in and out, using the crowd for cover, and Clint was not able to get off a shot. Suddenly, however, one of them veered off, and the other turned and stared after him, unsure of what to do.

"Hold it!" Clint shouted.

The shooter saw him and raised his gun. The people on the street—city people, but savvy enough to know when trouble was brewing—ducked out of the way or simply dropped to the ground. The man pointed his gun at Clint, but was way too slow. Clint fired once. He saw the bullet strike the man in the chest in a burst of red.

The man staggered back, his mouth open, and then red flowed from there, too, and he died, his body dropping to the ground.

Clint continued running until he reached the fallen man. He waited until he had kicked the gun away from the body—just in case he wasn't quite dead—then looked around for the second man, but he was gone.

Clint looked down at the first man and didn't recognize him. He knew one thing for sure, though. Killing this man on a busy Manhattan street was not going to make one Lieutenant Egan very happy.

THIRTY-NINE

"I'm not happy with you, Adams!" Egan snapped.

They were in his office at Police Headquarters, and the door was closed.

"Not happy at all."

"I can't say that I blame you, Lieutenant," Clint said, "but they shot at me first."

"So you chase them down a busy street and exchange shots with them? This is not Dodge City!"

"Begging your pardon, Lieutenant," Clint said, "but I chased them down a busy street and fired one shot, straight and true, before either of them could fire one. No one was endangered."

"That's your way of lookin' at it."

"That's how it happened."

Lieutenant Egan sat back in his chair, which creaked beneath his weight.

"Who were they?"

"I don't know."

"Why were they shootin' at you?"

"I don't know that, either."

"What do you know?"

"I think it has something to do with Annie Oakley, and with Frank Butler."

"Something to do with Butler being attacked?"

"Yes."

"So you think the same man shot at you?"

"I think they were sent by him," Clint said, "sent by Vernon Weeks to kill me, get me out of the way."

"This Vernon Weeks, is he an old enemy of yours?"

"No," Clint said, "I never heard of him until I came to New York."

"What does he want with Annie Oakley, then?" Egan asked.

"I don't know," Clint said, "all I know is that when she goes out alone, he's there, and he follows her."

"Which is not against the law."

"He made a threat to Butler, and he attacked him."

"Butler can't identify him."

"He heard his voice."

"But didn't see his face." Egan frowned. "This isn't gettin' us anywhere. You don't know the man you killed?"

"No," Clint said. "You can't identify him?"

"Not yet," Egan said. "Aren't you used to killin' men you don't know?"

"That's not something you ever get used to, Lieutenant."

Egan walked Clint to the front door.

"I probably shouldn't let you walk out of here," he said. "The city would be better off if I kept you here."

"You can't arrest me," Clint said. "I didn't do anything illegal."

"You fired a gun on the street."

Clint thought about that. The only gun he'd had with him was his New Line, and it had taken a perfect shot with that small gun to kill the shooter.

"In self-defense."

"I could make a case against that," Egan said, "but I won't."

"That's decent of you, Lieutenant."

"No," Egan said, "I'm just thinkin' that havin' you on the street might draw out that second shooter—or the man they work for."

"In which case," Clint said, "they'll get killed, or I will."

"And I'll arrest the survivor."

"So you're just going to watch?" Clint asked. "You could put a man on the Waldorf to keep an eye on Annie Oakley."

"Like Owens?" Egan asked. "He's got himself a bad crush on Miss Oakley."

"Yeah, it could be Owens."

"The kid will end up gettin' himself killed," Egan said. "I can't spare the manpower, Adams."

"You could if you wanted to."

"Well," Egan said, "then maybe I don't want to." The lieutenant turned and walked away, and Clint went out the door.

●　　●　　●

The second man walked into the Bowery bar and found Vernon Weeks sitting there.

"You're alone?" Weeks asked.

"I'm alive."

"I see," Weeks said. "You failed."

"I didn't fail," the man said. "I wasn't the one who made the mistakes."

"I understand," Weeks said. "Why would you serve under a man like that, anyway?"

"Money."

"I'll pay you all the money you want."

"I'll need help," the second man said. "Several good men."

"Get them, then," Weeks said. "I want Clint Adams out of my way—and if you can get rid of that Brooklyn detective, too, I'll pay extra."

The second man smiled and said, "Consider it done."

FORTY

Clint went back to the Waldorf to check on Annie and Frank Butler. If an attempt had been made on him, there might have been one on them, too. He walked quickly through the lobby and up to their room. When he knocked, the door was opened by Delvecchio, with a gun in his hand.

"It's you," the detective said. "Checking up on me?"

"Checking on all of you," Clint said. "I just killed one of two men who tried to kill me."

"Come on in and tell us about it," Delvecchio said, backing away from the door.

Clint entered and told them all the incidents of the past couple of hours . . .

"How could Lieutenant Egan blame you for this?" Annie asked when he was done.

"He was just being difficult," Clint said. "It's the relationship he and I have formed in our previous encounters."

"He's not exactly upholding the law," Butler said, "just sitting back and waiting for you and Weeks to kill each other."

"If we did that," Clint said, "it would make his job a lot easier."

"That's a horrible way to think," Annie said.

"I know Egan," Delvecchio said. "It's the only way he can think."

"What will Weeks do now that you killed one of his men?" Butler asked.

"If I was him," Clint said, "I'd replace him . . . with three or more."

"Sounds like you're gonna need some more help, Clint," Delvecchio said.

"I'll let you know, Delvecchio," Clint said. "For now I just wanted to make sure you were all safe. Lock the door after me."

"Where are you going?" Annie asked.

"I'm not sure," Clint said.

"I am," Delvecchio said. "Wait a minute." He went to a writing desk in the corner and used it. When he returned to Clint's side he handed him a slip of paper with a name and address on it—a Brooklyn address.

"Who's Jack Po?"

"A friend of mine," Delvecchio said, "that is, a colleague. We used to be friends. I don't know if we are anymore."

"Another Brooklyn detective?" Clint asked.

"That's right."

"Why do I want to talk to him?"

"Because," Delvecchio said, "he might know something about Vernon Weeks."

"You remembered something?"

"Only the name Weeks, which I still can't place," Delvecchio said, "but I think I heard it from Jack."

"Okay," Clint said, "okay, I'll go and see Jack Po tomorrow. Maybe he knows something that will help. Thanks."

."And tonight?" Annie asked.

"Tonight we have dinner with Cody, remember? To sign the papers?"

"Oh, God," she said, "and that's in less than an hour." She grabbed her head. "I have to get ready." She rushed from the room.

"I'll see you down in the restaurant," Clint said. "Delvecchio, you'll be eating with us."

"Thanks," he said, "but I think I'll get my own table. It'll make less of a crowd at your table, and I'll be able to watch the whole room."

"Okay," Clint said, "it's your job. Frank, see you later."

Delvecchio walked Clint to the door and stepped out into the hall with him.

."I was going to ask you if you were armed when I got here, but you answered that question when I walked in. What kind of a gun is that?"

"German," Delvecchio said, taking the weapon from a shoulder rig under his jacket. "A Borchardt German Luger, brand-new. Holds nine rounds."

"Impressive," Clint said. He hefted the weapon and handed it back. "Let Annie and Frank have a look at it sometime."

"I will," Delvecchio said, reholstering the weapon. "Where are you going now?"

"Well," Clint said, "to take a page out of Annie's book, I'm going to go and get dressed for dinner."

"I didn't bring any clothes," Delvecchio said. "I didn't know I'd be staying overnight."

"I'll have the hotel send something up," Clint said. He took Delvecchio's size.

"Nothing too fancy," the detective said. "I wouldn't want to have to live up to the quality of my clothes."

"Don't worry," Clint said. "I'll see you later."

He left, and Delvecchio went back inside.

Clint went down to the desk and asked the desk clerk to have a couple of jackets and some trousers sent up to the honeymoon suite, and gave him the size.

"Charge it to Colonel Cody's room."

He didn't know this clerk, but the man said, "Right away, Mr. Adams."

True to his word, the hotel manager had obviously arranged for Clint to get whatever he wanted on Cody's bill. He made a note to try not to take advantage of that.

FORTY-ONE

When Clint came down for dinner, he found he was the last one to arrive. Annie and Butler were sitting at a table with Cody, and Delvecchio—as he had promised—had gotten his own table near the door. From there he could not only monitor the room, but who came and went.

As Clint entered the dining room, though—exchanging a nod with the detective—he was surprised to see two additional people at Annie and Frank's table—Nate Salsbury and Mae Sinclair.

Mae's appearance was the biggest—and nicest—surprise of all. Nate, of course, was Cody's contract man, so it made sense that he was there. But Mae . . . Clint couldn't figure Mae's attendance at the dinner, and neither could Annie. It was obvious from the look on her face.

As Clint approached the table, he saw that Mae was

seated between Cody and an empty chair where Clint was obviously supposed to sit. He wondered if Cody knew what had happened between him and Mae that afternoon, and was possibly going to try to use it to his advantage—except that Clint had already agreed to sign.

"There he is," Cody said, as if they'd just been talking about him. "Clint, I think you remember Mae."

"I do," Clint said. "Hello."

"I saved you a seat next to me," Mae said, with a smile.

"Thank you."

Clint took a moment to shake hands with Nate Salsbury, who was sitting right across from him. He then sat next to Mae, who was wearing a low-cut dress she might have worn, at one time, on a stage. Since Annie was dressed in a much simpler fashion, he knew that this must also be bothering her.

When he sat, he was immediately aware of the heat Mae's body was giving off. He wondered if she was always this hot, or was it especially in his honor?

"We waited for you to order," Mae said, leaning toward him and engulfing him not only in her heat, but her heady scent.

"Thank you."

"I tried to get Delvecchio to sit with us," Butler said, "but he refused."

"He's doing his job," Clint said.

"Which one is the detective?" Mae asked, putting her hand on Clint's arm.

"The man sitting by the door."

"He's very handsome."

"I'll tell him you said so."

"Why don't you go and sit with him?" Annie asked Mae, sweetly. "He looks a little lonely."

"Colonel Cody invited me to dine here, at this table," she replied, just as sweetly. "It would be rude of me to leave."

The waiter, seeing that all the seats were now filled, came to take their order. Cody made sure to tell him to see what the man seated by the door wanted and add it to their check. The waiter took their orders—all steaks, except for Mae's chicken—and then went to take Delvecchio's, as well.

"Steak is a specialty here," Annie said to Mae. "I'm surprised you ordered chicken."

"I don't eat red meat," Mae said. "It's bad for my skin. As someone who is a performer, I like to take care of my skin."

"I think your skin is lovely," Nate Salsbury said.

"Really?" Annie asked.

Nate, flustered now, looked at Annie and said, "Oh, uh, you have lovely skin, too, Annie."

"Thank you, Nate," Annie said, but there was no thanks in her tone. She was still glaring across the table at Mae, who obviously only had eyes for Clint. It was also obvious to Clint that Salsbury was very sweet on Mae Sinclair. He hoped this would not cause a problem during the four weeks he was going to be in servitude to Cody.

"Clint, Annie," Cody said, "Nate has redrawn up the papers with the changes you—er, Frank—requested. I have them right here. Why don't we get them signed before the table fills up with greasy plates?"

On cue Nate withdrew the papers from his jacket pocket and passed them to Clint and Annie.

"I was very happy to hear you were joining us," Mae said, leaning into Clint. She managed to press a shoulder to his shoulder and a hip to his hip. Then, while he was signing his name, she slid a hand into his lap, which almost made him go off the page with the last letter.

Annie signed her name and they both passed the contracts to Cody, who also signed. The papers then went back to Nate Salsbury, who put them back in his pocket. Mae's hand, however, stayed where it was, squeezing Clint's thigh and causing an uncontrollable but very understandable physical reaction.

"Well, now that's done and we can eat," Cody said. "I think I'll order a bottle of champagne for a toast."

"Oh, I love champagne!" Mae said, simultaneously digging her nails into Clint's thigh.

He kept himself from jumping in his seat and said, "Never cared for it much, myself. But I'll drink a toast."

With six people at the table, it was natural that conversations would break into units, and Mae seemed intent on keeping her and Clint as a separate unit.

"I was so glad when the Colonel invited me," she said, so only he could hear her. "I really enjoyed meeting you this afternoon."

"Yes," Clint said, "I kind of enjoyed it myself."

He decided there was no harm in leaving Mae's hand right where it was—until it ventured further, found him hard, and began to stroke him. At that point he placed his napkin on his lap and firmly removed her hand from his penis—but left it on his thigh.

Then he decided that two could play at that game. He slid his left hand over to her thigh, found it hot to the touch, and left it there until the champagne came.

FORTY-TWO

"A toast to our newest act," Cody said, raising his glass after the waiter had filled them all, "Annie Oakley and The Gunsmith!"

"Here, here," Mae said. "I'll drink to The Gunsmith."

The snub of Annie was obvious and Clint saw Frank Butler put his hand on Annie's arm before she could make some remark.

They drank the toast and then the waiter came with the dinner plates. Clint needed both hands to cut his steak, so he had to take his left one from Mae's solid, hot thigh. Mae needed both hands for her chicken, so Clint was able to eat his dinner without an erection.

"So tell us what this new act is going to do, Colonel Cody," Mae said.

"What it's gonna do?" Cody asked. "It's gonna shoot bull's-eyes, Mae. That's what."

"It should make us a lot of money, too," Nate said, "a lot of money for everyone."

"Well, that sounds good," Mae said. "Why have they only signed for a four-week run, then?" Mae looked directly across the table at Annie. "Don't you like to make money?"

"There are extenuating circumstances that we won't discuss," Butler said, before Annie could say a word.

"I see."

"But I'm working on it," Cody said.

For the rest of the meal Cody regaled them with tales not of his days as a scout or a buffalo hunter, but his early days as a showman. Mae's hands had gotten slightly greasy from the chicken, so she had not put one back into Clint's lap. Clint was both pleased and disappointed.

The stories went on through dessert and then the waiter brought the check and handed it to Cody. He signed it so that the amount would be added to his room bill.

"Well," Cody said, "that was a fine meal, with good company, and we accomplished something. All in all very enjoyable. I'm going to go to the bar for a cigar and a drink. Would any of you gents care to join me?"

"I will, Colonel," Salsbury said.

"So will I," Clint said.

"No ladies allowed?" Mae asked. "Maybe Annie and I should go have a cigarette and a drink somewhere."

"I don't think so," Annie said, coldly. "I have a headache."

"Comin' to the bar, Frank?" Cody asked.

"No," Butler said, "I think I'll take Annie up to our room. If you'll excuse us, we'll say good night here."

They all stood, and while Annie and Frank were saying good night to Cody and Salsbury, Mae slid her hand into one of Clint's pockets.

"What are you doing?" he asked.

"Looking for your key," she said, "so I don't have to take a cab ride alone back to my own hotel."

"You're not staying here?"

"The Colonel wouldn't get me a room here," she said. "But as to whether or not I'm staying here tonight, that's up to you."

Clint didn't hesitate. He fished his key out of his pocket and pressed it into her palm.

"Don't be long," she whispered.

They all left the dining room together, Delvecchio accompanying Annie and Butler to their room. Salsbury asked Mae if she needed help getting a cab to her hotel, but she told him she was fine. She waited until he, Cody and Clint had gone into the bar to go up to Clint's room and let herself in with his key.

Cody and Salsbury each got a brandy from the bartender while Clint just had a beer. He did, however, accept one of Cody's cigars, and all three men stood at the bar and lit them.

"Nothin' like a good cigar, eh, Clint?" Cody asked.

"Unless it's a good woman," Salsbury said.

"Got a particular woman in mind, Nate?" Cody asked.

"No, sir," Salsbury said. "Just making a comment."

"A cigar is just an occasional thing with me," Clint said. "You probably shouldn't have wasted this one on me, Bill."

"Nonsense," Cody said. "Plenty more where that came

from. Tell me, Clint, when will you be ready to come out and rehearse?"

"I don't know," Clint said. "I guess we better check with Annie and see when we're ready."

"We have to work up an act," Cody said, "something the crowd will really like."

"I thought we were just going to shoot against each other," Clint said.

"There has to be more to it than that," Cody said, "much more."

"It has to be a show," Salsbury said.

"Well, Colonel," Clint said, "I guess I'll have to defer to you and Annie on that. You two are the experts." He finished his beer. He wanted to put out the cigar, but didn't want to do it in front of Cody. "I'll be turning in now."

"Got somethin' sweet waitin' for you, Clint?" Cody asked.

"Yes, I do, Cody," Clint replied. "My pillow."

He decided to put the cigar out after all.

FORTY-THREE

Clint stopped at the front desk to get a second key. The clerk did not bother to ask him why he needed it; he just handed it over. Clint used the key to let himself into his darkened room. Just inside the door he stopped and put his hand on his gun. After all, he didn't know Mae Sinclair all that well, except for a few minutes romping in a tent and a two-hour dinner with her hand in his lap.

There was a light in the bedroom so he moved toward it. He'd noticed the day before that the scent of the last woman he'd had in there—Karyn Walker—had finally faded away. Now, as he approached the bedroom, he could smell Mae Sinclair in the air.

"Is that you, Clint?" her voice called.

"It's me," Clint said.

"Well, come on in," she invited. "It's your bedroom, and I've been waiting for you."

He moved his hand away from his gun. He had a sixth sense that went off when danger was near, and at that moment it was telling him nothing.

As he entered the room, he saw Mae lying in his bed, beneath a sheet which molded itself to her body—as she had intended. He could see the swell of her belly and breasts, and her hard nipples.

"It's about time," she said. "After this afternoon I'm impatient to get you into a real bed. When the Colonel invited me to dinner, I knew I'd have my chance."

Clint unbuckled his gunbelt, walked around and hung it on the bedpost. Her eyes followed every move he made. He unbuttoned his shirt, removed it and dropped it to the floor, then divested himself of his boots, socks, trousers and underwear.

"Oh my," she said. She reached out and stroked his already hard penis. "I never did get to see it in that tent, did I?"

"Oh, I don't know," he said. "I seem to remember being in your mouth."

"Oh yes." She shivered. "I do seem to remember that. I think I had my . . . eyes closed at the time." She smiled dreamily. "I was just using my sense of . . . taste."

He felt his heartbeat quicken as she spoke, and stroked him very lightly. When she touched a place just beneath the mushroom head of his cock, he couldn't help but twitch.

Instead of letting her call the tune, he decided to take the initiative. He reached down, grasped the edge of the sheet right between her full breasts and then whipped it off her.

"Oh!" she said.

Her body was not as overly full and lush as Karyn Walker's had been. She was as tall as the other woman, but her body was . . . sleeker, even though her breasts and hips were full.

He put his hands on her and ran them down her body, cupping her breasts, flicking the nipples with his thumb. She caught her breath and bit her lip as he ventured down further, to her belly and abdomen. She arched her back when his hand moved into the hair between her legs, and she groaned when his middle finger slid along her moist slit. Actually, it was more of a growl, and convulsively she reached down, grabbed his wrist and pressed his hand more tightly to her.

"I can't wait . . . ," she said. "Come to bed."

He got into the bed with her, inserted his finger deep inside her, making her breath catch again, and then withdrew his finger and—while staring into her eyes—very deliberately put it in his mouth to suck her juices from it.

"Oh God," she said, "that is so . . . nasty! I love it."

She grabbed his hand, brought the finger to her own mouth and sucked it in.

"Mmmm," she said, sucking and then licking it off. "You and me, we combine to make a great flavor."

He lay down next to her and kissed her. Her mouth was anxious, her tongue alive in his mouth. Once again his hands roamed over her body, and he couldn't help but compare her to the other woman. Her breasts were easily as full as Karyn's had been, but harder, firmer. She was probably younger than the other woman by several years, and—used to being on display—she kept her body in better shape. Both women, however, were sexy, sensual beings who came alive in bed, and had few—if any—inhibitions.

Lying to her left side, he kissed her breasts while once again caressing and touching her pussy. She moaned and writhed on the bed and said in a guttural tone, "If you don't put it in me now, I'm going to go crazy."

"Well," he said, "I wouldn't want that to happen."

He slid his leg over her and straddled her. Making her wait a little longer, he slid his penis along her smooth belly, then down into her hair. His erection was extremely sensitive, and it was as if he could feel each individual hair.

"Ooh God, you beautiful bastard, you're making me wait," she scolded him. She reached for him, pulled his face down to her breasts. He lifted his hips, probed the wet lips of her pussy teasingly, then slid into her roughly, causing her to gasp, her eyes to go wide.

"Oh," she said, "yes!"

FORTY-FOUR

Delvecchio stood at the window and stared out at Park Avenue.

"What are you thinking?" Annie asked from behind him.

He turned, saw her walking toward him.

"I thought you and Frank went to bed."

"Frank's asleep," she said. "I couldn't."

She'd pulled on a pair of pants and a shirt, and come out of the bedroom barefoot. As she walked toward him, he noticed how her breasts moved, indicating that she had no underwear beneath her shirt.

She came up and stood beside him, in front of the window.

"Would you move to the side, please?" he asked her. "You're too good a target standing where you are."

"Oh." She took two steps to her left. "Is this better?"

"Much."

"I don't think Vernon Weeks wants to kill me," she said. "At least, not yet. He's had plenty of opportunities."

"Just the same," he said, "I like to be safe."

"You haven't answered my question."

"About what?"

"What were you thinkin' when I came out?"

"Actually," he said, "my mind was a complete blank. I was leaving myself open to whatever was out there."

"You can do that?"

"Sometimes."

"I wish I could," she said. "I'd be able to sleep if I could turn off my brain."

"I noticed there's a small bar over there with some brandy on it," he said. "How about a glass? That might help you sleep."

"Will you have one with me?"

"Sure," he said. "I'll get it." He started away, then stopped. "Don't move back in front of the window."

"I won't," she said. "I promise."

Vernon Weeks sighted down the barrel of his rifle. From the roof across the way he could see the Waldorf clearly, and he knew which windows were the honeymoon suite. There was a light on in one of them, and he could clearly see the man standing in the window. Eventually, another figure moved into the window, then out of it. He knew it was Annie Oakley.

He watched and waited. The male figure in the window was backlit, but Weeks wasn't interested in him as a target. He hadn't picked out his target yet, but suddenly there it was, on the windowsill. Weeks had eyes like a cat; it was what made him such a good marksman.

He put those eyes to very good use now.

Delvecchio went to the sidebar, poured two small glasses of brandy and returned to the window.

"Thank you," Annie said, as he handed her one. "So how long have you known Clint?"

"I guess you could say I've known him for a couple of years," he said. "We met the last time he was in New York, but I haven't seen him since. And you?"

"He's a friend of Frank's," she said. "They've known each other a long time. I just met him a few days ago, but already I feel like we're good friends."

"Yeah," Delvecchio said, "he does that. I don't know how. I mean, I'm a pretty cynical guy, but I think he's one of the best people I've ever met."

"Exactly!" she said. "I don't know how he does it, either."

They sipped their brandy and stared out the window. Just in an attempt to break the silence, Delvecchio told her that Clint had wanted him to show her his German gun. He handed it to her and she turned it over in her hands, admiring it. She asked a few questions, which he answered, and then she handed it back.

"It's a fine weapon," she said.

"Thanks."

She'd had to put her glass down on the windowsill to look the gun over, and now she started to reach down to pick it up. Abruptly a bullet punched a hole through the window and shattered the glass before she could grab it.

"Get down!" the detective shouted. He dropped his glass, tackled, brought her to the floor.

"What the hell—" Frank Butler shouted. He came running out of the bedroom, gun in hand.

"Down, Frank!" Delvecchio called out.

Butler immediately hit the floor.

"What happened?" he demanded.

"A shot," Delvecchio said.

"Just one?"

"So far. You two stay down."

German pistol in hand, Delvecchio made his way back to the window, keeping very low until he reached it, then risked a look outside. When nothing happened, he stood up slowly.

"Delvecchio," Annie said, "be careful."

The detective stood all the way up, making a fine target of himself, but then said, "I think he's gone."

"Just one shot?" Butler asked, getting to his feet. "And he missed?" He helped Annie up and hugged her.

Delvecchio looked down at the shattered remnant of the brandy glass on the floor. He had not filled brandy snifters, but rather the smaller glasses that he knew were to be used for other liquors.

"Damn," he said.

"What are you thinking?" Butler asked.

"I think he was on the roof across the way," Delvecchio said. "I didn't hear a shot, but that building's roof is even with this window."

"Weeks is a good shot," Butler said. "How did he miss?"

"Annie was standing to the side," Delvecchio said, "but I was a clear target."

"Like I said," Butler repeated, "how did he miss?"

"I don't think he did."

"What do you mean?" Annie asked.

"You put your glass on the windowsill," Delvecchio said. He'd placed his own there, as well, and now he picked it up to show it to Annie and Butler. "I don't think he hit it by accident."

Butler released Annie, approached Delvecchio and took the small glass from him.

"You think he hit this on purpose?"

"It was backlit," Delvecchio said. "He could probably make out the color."

Butler looked at Annie.

"That was a damn fine shot," he said. "I don't know if I could have made it. You probably could've, but I don't know about me."

"He had to hit the glass without hitting Delvecchio," she said. "That was a damn fine shot."

"From a man you've already beaten several times?" Delvecchio asked.

Butler handed the glass back to the detective. He went to the sidebar, filled two snifters halfway this time, then took one to Annie and retained the other one.

"Maybe," he said, looking at Annie, "you didn't beat him at all."

"What are you saying?" Delvecchio asked. "That he lost to Annie on purpose?"

"Anybody who could make that shot from across the street, at night," Butler said, "is a helluva shot."

Delvecchio looked down at himself, saw that the brandy had stained his shirt and pants in some places. It had been that close.

A helluva shot, indeed.

FORTY-FIVE

Mae Sinclair turned out to be a rough ride.

Clint had to hold onto her for dear life because as he began fucking her, Mae got increasingly more . . . excited. Or maybe agitated was a better word. When he thought about it later, he wasn't sure, but at the time he couldn't think about it because she began to buck beneath him so violently he would have thought she was trying to throw him off but for the fact she had her arms and legs wrapped around him.

"Ooh, Jesus, ooh God, yeah . . ." she said, into his ear. "That's it, faster, come on, harder . . . harder!"

Their skin became damp with sweat, making them stick together in places—or they would have if they'd stopped moving, which they never did.

She was so tight it was like she was sucking him, and

he didn't know if that was natural, or if she had that much control over her muscles. Whatever it was, it made for an unbelievable sensation. He slid his hands beneath her so he could hold tightly to her buttocks—again noticing that while she was roughly the size of Karyn Walker, she was considerably firmer.

Her already deep voice became more and more guttural the longer they went at each other, and finally she seemed to grow hoarse, or dry. She stopped talking to him and simply began to grunt. Then he could feel her beginning to tremble as her time grew near . . . and he fought free of her and withdrew.

"Wha—wha—" she stammered. "What are you doing? Why did you stop?"

"Just lie there and see," he said.

He slithered down between her legs and pressed his mouth to her wet, fragrant, sweet mound. He delved into her with his tongue and licked her up and down for a few moments before centering on her rigid clit. She jerked her hips, either in appreciation or surprise, and then she reached down to cup the back of his head with both hands and began to move her hips in unison with his mouth and tongue. She had already been near her orgasm, so it didn't take much of this to push her over the edge, and when she went, she did not go quietly . . .

Her cries had not died down yet when he got up onto his knees again, spread her legs forcefully and drove into her again.

"Oh, God!" she said, hoarsely. "Jesus . . . you're gonna kill me. Don't stop!"

He kissed her deeply, then laughed and said against her mouth, "Oh, I have no intention of stopping."

•   •   •

Later she was lying down between his outstretched legs, playing with his penis.

"I told you," he said, "you wore me out. There's nothing left down there."

"You are the prettiest man down here," she said, sliding her fingers up and down him. She leaned forward and kissed the tip, then slid it into her mouth. Immediately he started to get hard.

She allowed him to pop free of her mouth and said, "You were lying to me."

"I wasn't lying," he said. "You just have the most incredible fingers and mouth."

She used two fingers to slide up and down his lengthening penis, examining it with almost clinical interest.

"So pretty," she said, almost to herself. She nuzzled him with her nose, then stuck out her tongue and ran it along the underside. His dick began to twitch uncontrollably.

"You're either going to have to come up here and mount up," he warned her, "or do something while you're down there."

She rubbed the ball of her thumb over the swollen head of his prick and said, "Don't be impatient. I'm enjoying myself down here."

"Well," he said, "far be it from me to interrupt your pleasure."

"I think," she said, cupping his heavy testicles in one hand, "we're dealing with your pleasure right now."

He let his head settle back on the pillow and said, "You'll get no argument from me."

That's when the knock came at the door.

FORTY-SIX

Clint toyed with the idea of ignoring the knock but finally decided he had to answer it.

"I'll be right back," he told Mae, pulling his pants on hastily.

Lying naked on the bed, on her belly, she grinned up at him and said, "I'm not going anywhere."

He admired the line of her back and the swell of her buttocks, then shook his head and made himself leave the room.

When he finally opened the door, he was sure he was glaring at Delvecchio.

"I was going to wait until morning," the man said, "but I thought I should tell you now. I hope I'm not interrupting anything."

"You are," Clint said, "but what are you talking about?"

"Can I come in?"

Clint nodded, backed up and allowed Delvecchio to enter. Once inside, the detective seemed to sniff the air and nod to himself. Briefly, he told Clint what had happened with the brandy glass.

"Annie and Frank were both impressed with the shot?" Clint asked.

"Oh yeah," Delvecchio said. "It was a damn good shot."

"He was just sending a message, then," Clint said.

"Which was what? That he could kill her anytime? Or any one of us at any time?"

"Or he was showing off."

"For Annie?"

Clint nodded. "Showing her that he was worthy of her, after all."

"Why didn't he just show her that by beating her in a contest or two?"

"Maybe he couldn't," Clint said. "Maybe those contests are Annie's specialty. Maybe he's good at a different kind of shooting. Who knows? I'll have to go and check on that roof tomorrow."

"For what?"

"Just to make sure it was him," Clint said, "if he left anything behind, that is."

"Like what?"

"Footprints," Clint said. "I saw some on the floor of the building across from Annie's old hotel. If they match . . ."

"Okay," Delvecchio said, "I get it. I better get back. I don't want to leave them alone for too long."

"Are they okay?"

"Annie's kind of shaken," Delvecchio said. "The bullet virtually passed between us."

"How are you doing?"

"I don't mind telling you I'm kind of shaken, myself," the detective admitted. "It was a hell of a shot."

"Maybe," Clint said, "it was an accident."

Delvecchio frowned.

"Maybe he was aiming for you."

"Oh . . . well . . . ," Delvecchio said, "leave it to you to say something comforting."

After Delvecchio left, Clint took a moment before returning to the bedroom. He was certain that shot had been deliberate. It was interesting to wonder about a man who could make a shot like that and yet lose some sharpshooting contests where the targets might have been easier. Maybe when he took the trip out to Brooklyn tomorrow to talk to Delvecchio's friend Jack Po, he'd find out something about the man.

"Clint?" Mae's voice called from the bedroom. Once again he felt that chill run down his spine.

"Do you want a drink?" Clint called back.

She laughed, a deep throaty laugh that made his penis twitch, and said, "I just want you to come back in here, lover, so we can finish what we started."

FORTY-SEVEN

In the morning Clint awoke and noticed that Mae was asleep all the way on the other side of the bed. Apparently, she was not one of those women who liked to sleep pressed right up against a man. He took a moment to admire her naked back and butt, then covered her with the sheet and got out of bed.

He succeeded in washing and dressing without waking her. He didn't wonder. They had worn each other out the night before, but oddly enough he felt refreshed. There's something to be said for spending the night with a beautiful, energetic, talented woman.

He let himself out, still without waking her, and went downstairs to have some breakfast alone.

He was finishing up his steak and eggs when Delvecchio, Annie and Butler all appeared.

"Mind if we join you?" Annie asked.

"I'm just finishing," he said, "but I'll have a cup of coffee with you."

They all sat down with him. Clint waved to the waiter to bring more coffee, which he did immediately, and then he took orders and withdrew.

"So how did everyone sleep after last night's display of marksmanship?" Clint asked.

"Not well," Annie said, "and I wasn't sleeping well before that. I can't imagine how Delvecchio felt on the sofa. Clint, can we see about getting him something else to sleep on?"

"I was just fine," Delvecchio said.

But Clint added, "I'll see what I can do."

"So what are we thinking about doing today?" Frank Butler asked the table at large.

"I'm going across the street to check on that rooftop," Clint said, "and then I have an errand to run in Brooklyn."

"What are we supposed to do?" Annie asked.

"You can do whatever you want," Clint said, "as long as you take Delvecchio with you. Annie, did Cody talk to you about coming up with an act?"

"No."

"Well, he asked me about it, and about when we'd be able to rehearse. I told him I'd leave that in your hands, and his."

"All right," Annie said. "I guess that's what we could do today, go out to Staten Island."

"That makes me uncomfortable," Delvecchio said. "It's way too open."

"If Weeks follows you out there, he'll have no place to hide," Clint pointed out.

"He could get Annie or Frank anywhere between here

and the ferry, Clint," he said, "not to mention me."

"Why would he want to shoot you?" Annie asked.

"Just to get me out of the way."

"He could have done that last night, and he didn't," Clint pointed out. "I think you're okay to go."

"Okay," Delvecchio said, "you're the boss."

"No," Clint said, "you're the one protecting them now. You make the final decision."

Clint looked at Annie and Butler. "Agreed?"

"Agreed," Annie said.

"It's okay by me," Butler said.

"I do have a favor to ask, though."

"What's that?" Butler asked.

"Could you give Mae Sinclair a ride out there?"

"What?" Annie said.

All three men looked at her.

"Don't tell me . . . ," she said, looking at Clint.

Chagrined, he said, "Okay, I won't."

She glared at all three of them then and just said, "Men!"

FORTY-EIGHT

Clint was sorry Annie was so angry about Mae, but he couldn't worry about that. She was Frank Butler's wife, not his. He simply wanted to make sure Mae got out to Staten Island safely. He wasn't going to apologize for that.

After breakfast he went across the street and found his way to the roof of the hotel there. All he found up there were footprints that matched the ones he'd previously found. According to Delvecchio, the shooter—probably Vernon Weeks—had fired only one shot. He had not left any shells behind—or anything else, for that matter. The man made sure he cleaned up after himself.

Too bad.

Clint went back across the street to the Waldorf and let the doorman get him a cab.

"Where are you going, sir?" he asked Clint.

"Brooklyn."

"I'd better get you a driver who won't leave you stranded out there, then."

"I'd appreciate that."

He tipped the man big.

The driver turned out to be a young man named Willis. Clint didn't know if that was his first or last name, and he didn't care. He had a carriage and a horse, and that was all Clint cared about.

"Brooklyn's a long ride," Willis said.

"I know that," Clint replied. "Do you know your way around out there?"

"Do I?" Willis asked, laughing. "I live out there."

"The doorman said I could trust you not to strand me out there," Clint said. "Is that true?"

"For a prearranged fee," Willis said, "you could hire me for the whole day."

"Fine," Clint said, "let's prearrange it."

Jack Po lived in a section of Brooklyn called Gravesend. It was way out in the southern part of Brooklyn, and Clint was glad he and Willis had come to a prearranged fee.

"This is the address you gave me," Willis said, pulling to a stop in front of a rundown one-story house. "I'll wait here."

Clint gave him a look.

"Hey," the young man said, "you only paid me half of our prearranged fee. I ain't goin' anywhere."

"Okay," Clint said.

He walked to the door and knocked. After a few moments the door was opened by a man roughly the same age as Delvecchio, but with sandy hair and mild eyes.

"Yes?"

"Jack Po?"

"Who's asking?"

"Clint Adams," he said. "Delvecchio told me you might be able to help me out."

"You paying?"

"Yes."

"Then I can help you," Po said. "Come on in."

Clint entered. The house was stuffy, but not what he would have called dirty. He followed the man to the back of the house, to a nook he obviously used as an office. Po seated himself behind a beat-up desk and motioned Clint to a chair.

"What can I do for you, Mr. Adams?" he asked. "By the way, I know who you are."

"Do you?"

"I'd have to be a fool not to," Po said. "I know your reputation, and I know of your alliance at one time with Teddy Roosevelt. I am impressed with you. That's for the record."

"Thanks," Clint said, "I think."

"Now tell me," Po said, "why did my friend Delvecchio send you to me?"

"To find out about a man named Weeks."

Po frowned. "Tyler Weeks?"

"I'm dealing with a man named Vernon Weeks," Clint said. "Any relation?"

"They were brothers. I lost track of Vernon after Tyler committed suicide."

"His brother killed himself?"

Po nodded. "Shot himself in the head."

"Why?"

"The Weeks brothers were considered the best marksmen in the East," Po said, "and they wanted to prove themselves out West. Tyler was the first to try."

"What happened?"

"Apparently poor Tyler had a weak character," Po said, then added, "no pun intended. He got beat by the same person two, three times. It crushed his confidence, then he grew depressed. Finally, he put a gun to his head and pulled the trigger. Couldn't miss that way."

"Jesus," Clint said. "What a stupid way to die."

"I agree."

"What about his brother?"

"Apparently, he was mentally stronger than his brother," Po replied, "but like I said, I lost track of him after his brother died. He left New York. I figured maybe he went West to avenge his brother."

"Well, he's back in New York now, and he's threatening a friend of mine."

"Why?"

"You tell me," Clint said.

Po shrugged. "How would I know?"

"Do you know who Tyler Weeks shot against, and lost to?" Clint asked.

"Sure," Po said. "Annie Oakley."

Clint just nodded.

FORTY-NINE

"Oh," Po said, "I get it."

"Yeah," Clint said, "so do I, now."

Apparently, Vernon Weeks had entered into contests against Annie Oakley to find out how good she was. At the same time, he lost on purpose so she wouldn't know how good he was.

"And now he's following her," Po said, "stalking her, scaring her, trying to wear her down before he kills her."

"Maybe," Clint said. "He's had plenty of chances to kill her, or her husband. I'm not quite sure what he's waiting for."

"The right time, maybe."

Clint also told Po that there'd already been one attempt on his own life.

"By Weeks?"

"No," Clint said, "he's hiring it done. I killed one man, and the other got away."

"So he'll come back, and with more men."

"Probably."

"Police involved?"

Clint nodded.

"Who?"

"Lieutenant Egan."

"I know Egan," Po said. "In his own way he's a pretty good policeman."

"Really?" Clint asked. "You really think that?"

"Oh, yeah," Po said. "I mean, he looks for shortcuts, and he's kind of crude, but he's nobody's puppet. He's not taking money from anyone that I know of."

"I'm surprised," Clint said. "He strikes me as an . . . opportunistic man."

"Let's just say he keeps his eye out for opportunities, but he upholds the law."

"He's just going to sit back and wait for me and Weeks to sort this out."

"That's what he says," Po said. He sat back and folded his arms. "So what have you got Delvecchio doing?"

"Protecting Annie and her husband."

"And what do you want me to do?"

"Well," Clint said, "I only wanted information, but maybe I need somebody to watch my back."

"Me?" Po asked. "Watch The Gunsmith's back?"

"Delvecchio vouched for you," Clint said. "Said you were a good man."

"He's right," Po said, "I am good."

"Then you're hired . . . if you want the job."

"Oh, I want the job," Po said. "When do we start?"

"Now," Clint said. "I've got a cab waiting outside."

"I'll get my coat," Po said, "and my gun, and we can go."

They left Po's house and walked out to the cab.

"Hey, Willis," Po said.

"Mr. Po."

"You know each other?" Clint asked.

"We've met," Po said. "We both live out here."

Clint looked at Willis.

"When we pulled up in front, why didn't you tell me you knew who Jack Po was?"

Willis looked down from his seat on the carriage, shrugged and said, "You never asked."

Po looked at Clint and said, "Bet he's got you there."

Clint shook his head and said, "Let's just get in."

They climbed into the back of the carriage.

"Where to, gents?"

"Back across the bridge," Clint said.

Vernon Weeks watched as Annie Oakley, Frank Butler and their protector, Delvecchio, left the Waldorf that morning, probably going out to Staten Island. Where else was there for them to go?

He let them go. He'd made his point last night. Let them think about it for a while.

It annoyed him that Annie Oakley didn't seem to remember his brother, Tyler. When you humiliate a man to the point that he's driven to suicide, you should remember him. He was going to make sure she never forgot him again—until the day she died. And that day was coming, only not soon. There was still plenty he had to do.

• • •

As they drove back into Manhattan something occurred to Clint.

"Do you know where Vernon and Tyler Weeks lived?" he asked Po.

"No," Po said. "I know it wasn't in Brooklyn, though."

"And did you know them personally?"

"I knew *of* them."

"As marksmen?"

"That was their hobby," Po said.

"What was their real job?"

Po looked at Clint. "The Weeks boys were killers for hire."

"Now, why doesn't that surprise me?"

FIFTY

The minute Clint and Jack Po stepped off the carriage in front of the Waldorf, lead started flying. Unfortunately for Willis, the driver, he was standing up at the time, and two chunks of lead slammed him in the back. He was knocked from the carriage to the ground. His horse panicked and took off running down Park Avenue.

From across the street five men started running toward the front of the hotel, firing their guns.

Clint hit the ground quickly, plucking the Colt New Line from his belt. He didn't fire, though, because he only had five shots and they were small caliber. If he was going to be effective, he had to wait until they got closer. Jack Po, on the other hand, pulled out a long-barreled Colt and started blazing away. Even while they were under fire,

Clint wondered how Po could walk with that hogleg stuck down his pants.

The five men advancing on Clint and Jack Po, firing their guns, knew that this had to happen fast. They were getting paid enough money to make the risk of a gunfight in broad daylight on a Manhattan street worth it. But they also knew that it had to be done quickly, before reinforcements came in the way of police.

Their target was Clint Adams, They Gunsmith. They knew that. The other man with him was of no consequence, was not even to be fired upon. But other people who happened to get hurt were of no concern to them. Their only concern was to earn their money by putting as much lead into Clint Adams as they possibly good, as quickly as they could.

But then again, they were dealing with The Gunsmith.

The front area of the Waldorf had turned into the Wild West. It was almost like a scene out of one of Buffalo Bill Cody's shows. Lead was flying every which way and people were ducking for cover. Clint's educated ears heard the sound of lead ricocheting off cement, lead breaking windows and—the worst sound of all—lead striking flesh. Jack Po was firing back at the advancing men, who must have been getting paid plenty to mount a frontal assault like this. Po didn't seem to be hitting anything, though, and he wasn't being hit, either. Clint knew the main target of the attack was definitely him. This was no random act. This was meant for him, and had been bought and paid for.

He had to do something drastic.

"You got more bullets for that thing?" he shouted at
Jack Po.

"Of course!"

"Well, load it up and give it here."

"But I'm—"

"Don't make me take it, Po!" Clint shouted.

The detective hurriedly reloaded and handed the gun
to Clint, who knew he had to put a stop to this before
other people got hurt. Already Willis was dead, and he
could see the doorman was down, clutching his shoulder,
and another man was lying facedown on the ground.

Clint took Po's hogleg in his left hand and his Colt
New Line in his right and got to his feet. In a shocking
move to everyone concerned he started toward the five
men, who were standing in the street now, blazing away.
Two of them had dropped to a knee to reload, but they
never got the bullets into the guns.

Clint began firing, and his fusillade was deadly. Every
shot struck home. The two kneeling men were struck once
each—one in the face, another in the neck—and they fell
over. The other three saw their companions fall, and
turned to increase their barrage. But Clint was locked in
now. He could hear the bullets whizzing past him, and he
felt one or two of them tug at his clothes. One might even
have taken some flesh with it. He couldn't be sure at that
moment, and he didn't have time to look, or to feel pain.

The people who had taken cover to watch the battle—
which now included a stunned Jack Po—watched in
amazement as Clint stood tall, firing with both hands,
dealing out death with every shot, until finally the five
men's bodies littered the streets.

At some point two uniformed policemen had heard the
shooting and come running. When they arrived, their own

guns out, they were greeted by the sight of The Gunsmith meting out death. Now that the shooting had stopped and it was eerily silent, one of them called out to Clint, "Drop those guns!"

Clint turned at the sound of the voice and held his fire when he saw the two policemen.

"You heard him," the other man said. "Drop 'em!" Both uniformed men were pointing their weapons at him, and he noticed that at least one man's hand was shaking.

"Take it easy," Clint said. "It's all over." He bent down and laid both guns on the ground, then showed the policemen his empty hands.

At that point the hotel manager came running out, shouting at the cops not to shoot, that they had the wrong man. It would all get sorted out in good time, Clint knew, and he'd probably have to deal with Egan again, but at least the shooting had stopped and nobody else was going to get hurt.

Today.

FIFTY-ONE

Stuart White, the hotel manager, along with some other witnesses, managed to convince the two policemen that Clint was a hero, that he had fired his gun and killed the five men in self-defense, and in the defense of others. While the officers seemed convinced, they said they still had to hold him until their superior arrived.

"That wouldn't be Lieutenant Egan, would it?" Clint asked them.

"Yes, sir, it is," one of them said.

"Do you know the lieutenant?" the other man asked.

"We're acquainted."

"Then you'll understand why we want to do the right thing," the first man said, "and not get him mad."

"I understand perfectly."

They asked Stuart if Clint could wait inside and

he said, "Of course. Mr. Adams is a valued guest of the hotel."

"How's your doorman?" Clint asked.

"He was hit in the shoulder. We have a doctor looking at him now. The poor driver of the carriage is dead."

"There was another man shot, wasn't there? I saw him lying on the ground."

"There are a lot of broken windows," Stuart said, "and some other damage, and a lot of frightened guests, but I don't see another injured man. Do you, Officers?"

"No," one of them said, "no one but the five dead men. Look, we have to close off the street until we can remove those men. Just wait inside for the lieutenant, Mr. Adams . . . if you would."

"Of course."

As Clint and Stuart turned to go inside, Jack Po came walking over.

"When do I get my gun back?" he asked.

"When the lieutenant gets here, I imagine," Clint said. "Egan?"

"That's right."

"I don't think I want to be here when he gets here."

"You can't leave," Stuart said, "you're a witness."

"Just watch me," Po said. He pulled Clint aside. "There's a bar called O'Herlihy's on Houston Street, off the Bowery. Meet me there when you're finished with Egan. Oh, and bring my gun."

Clint was tempted to say, "I don't know why; you didn't hit anything with it," but instead he said, "Fine."

Po melted away and Clint entered the lobby with the manager.

"Mr. Adams," Stuart said, "if you'll have a seat, I'll have our doctor look at you."

"What?"

"You appear to be wounded, sir."

Clint looked down and saw some blood on the side of his shirt. He probed for a moment, then announced, "I lost some meat, but it's not bad. I could use a bandage, though."

"Yes, sir," Stuart said. "I'll send the doctor right over."

Clint sat down on one of the sofas in the Waldorf lobby. There were some bullet holes in the back of it, and the floor of the lobby was covered with shattered glass. He knew Egan was going to blame him for everything, but he wasn't about to accept it. He couldn't help but wonder how much Vernon Weeks had paid those men to do such a brazen thing. In Dodge City or Tombstone it might make sense, but on a New York street?

Vernon Weeks wanted him dead real bad—but when would he want it bad enough to try and take care of it himself?

By the time Egan walked in, crunching glass beneath his feet, the doctor had bandaged Clint's side.

"You'll live," the physician told him. "Just don't make any sudden moves."

"How many other people were hurt, Doctor?"

"Some folks had cuts from the glass; one woman lost an earlobe to a bullet, if you can believe that."

"You didn't see another injured man outside?"

"Only the doorman," the doctor said, "and I sent him to the hospital. Excuse me."

The doctor walked away, and Lieutenant Egan walked in and crunched his way to Clint.

"I understand you're responsible for this," the policeman said.

"If that's your information, then you were misinformed," Clint said. "I don't think anybody told you that."

"No," Egan said, "what I'm bein' told is that you're a hero. That you stood in the middle of the street with a gun in each hand and killed five crazy men who were shooting up the street."

"That's what happened."

Egan kicked at some of the glass on the floor.

"I'm thinkin' they weren't just shootin' up the street, Adams," he said. "I'm thinkin' they were shootin' at you."

"Well," Clint said, "I was there and they were shooting. I wasn't about to stand by and do nothing while innocent people got hurt. So I dealt myself a hand."

"And you happened to have two guns on you?"

Clint didn't answer, so Egan sat down next to him.

"Why don't you take me through this step by step?"

FIFTY-TWO

Instead of trying to explain how he happened to have two guns on him, Clint decided to take the offensive.

"What are you going to do about citizens getting gunned down in the streets?" he demanded.

"Only one I can see got gunned down was that poor cabbie, and the doorman," Egan said. "And judging from the blood on your shirt, you. Anybody else I should know about?"

"Like who?"

"Like whoever else got out of the cab with you?" Egan asked. "Like whoever else was shooting back at those men before you took his gun away from him and did your Wyatt Earp at the O.K. Corral impersonation? You want to tell me who that was?"

"I don't know," Clint said. "Just a man I shared the

227

cab with. And yes, when the shooting started, he shot
back, but he wasn't hitting anything. So I took his gun
away from him and took care of matters myself."

"You impressed the hell out of my officers," Egan said.
"They say you didn't waste one shot."

"There wasn't one to waste," Clint said, "and I've got
a question for you."

"What?"

"Why are so many of your officers young and inex-
perienced?" Clint asked.

"There's a youth movement goin' on in the depart-
ment," Egan said. "It's not somethin' I agree with, but
I've got to work with it, unless I want to retire."

"Are they trying to retire you, Egan?"

"It would make things a little easier for some people,
yes," the lieutenant said. "But we're not here to talk about
me, Adams."

"Lieutenant," Clint said, "what can I tell you? I got
down from the cab and these crazy men came running
across the street, shooting. Were they shooting at me?
Yes, among other people. I didn't stop to ask if I was the
main target. I did what I had to do."

Egan stared at Clint, then stood up. Behind him a man
came into the lobby, looked around anxiously and then
rushed over to where Clint and Egan were standing.

"Lieutenant, is that him?" the little man asked. "Is that
the man who killed the five gunmen?"

Egan turned to look at the man who was speaking.

"Jonesy," he said. "What took you so long to get here?
Clint Adams, Inkspot Jones. Jonesy works for the *Morning Telegraph*. I have no doubt he'd like to make you
more famous than you already are."

"A pleasure to meet you, Mr. Adams," Jonesy said.

"Inkspot?" Clint asked.

Egan shrugged.

"I used to do obituaries," the newspaperman explained. "Always had ink on me."

"Lieutenant—"

"Don't go away, Adams," Egan said. "I'm gonna get the street cleaned up and then come back to talk some more. Why don't you and Jonesy go into the bar and talk? I'll find you there."

As Egan walked away, Inkspot Jones started peppering Clint with questions.

"Mr. Jones, are you on an expense account?" Clint asked, cutting him off.

"Huh? Oh, sure."

"Come on, then," Clint said. "You buy the beer."

Clint headed for the bar, and the shorter man had to trot along to keep up.

They were seated in the bar, each with a beer, when Clint said, "Go ahead and ask your questions and I'll answer them as best I can."

Clint knew that Cody would love the publicity, but he was thinking of another man reading the account of what had happened. He was thinking maybe he could encourage Vernon Weeks to do his own dirty work, next time.

Word had spread fast of Clint's feat—singlehandedly gunning down five men with two guns—and the other men in the saloon were watching the interview take place.

"Who were those men, Mr. Adams?"

"They were paid assassins, Mr. Jones," Clint said, "hired by a coward who is afraid to face me himself."

"Do you know who this coward is?"

"His name is Vernon Weeks," Clint said.

Jones couldn't write fast enough. "What did you, uh, do to Mr. Weeks to make him want you dead, Mr. Adams?"

"I didn't do anything to him," Clint said. "He's trying to make a name for himself, but you can't do that by hiring others to do your work for you. The only way he's going to get a name is to face me himself."

"Mr. Adams—"

"Vernon Weeks," Clint said to Jones. "You got that?"

"I have it, sir," Jones said. "Now, Mr. Adams, how many men does this make that you've ki—"

"Interview's over, Inkspot," Clint said, abruptly. "Drink your beer."

FIFTY-THREE

Jones tried apologizing for his last question, but Clint had said all he had to say. If Jones wanted to print anything attributable to him, it would have to be what he said about Vernon Weeks.

Then he remembered Cody.

"I've got something else for you, Mr. Jones," Clint said.

"What's that?" the man asked, anxiously.

"I'll be appearing as part of Buffalo Bill's Wild West Show for four weeks, once his show opens on Staten Island."

"Really?" Jones asked. "When does it open?"

"You'll have to talk to Buffalo Bill or his man Nate Salsbury about that, Jonesy. I don't have the dates handy."

"What will you be doing—"

"Shooting," Clint said, "I'll be shooting."

Jones's eyes went wide.

"We've had reports that Annie Oakley is in New York and might be going back to Cody's Wild West Show after a long break. Can you confirm that?"

"I can't," Clint said. "Nate Salsbury's your man."

Clint saw Egan enter, spot Clint and then push his way past some of the bar's wealthy clientele, who were still pointing at Clint and talking among themselves.

"Jonesy," Clint said, "why don't you get the lieutenant a beer? He looks like he needs one."

"Huh? Oh, sure."

As Jones took off for the bar, Egan took his vacated seat.

"Get those men off the street?" Clint asked.

"Yes, we did."

"Any idea who they are?"

"Hired guns," Egan said. "Not the kind you've dealt with where you come from, but deadly enough."

"Would you say they were . . . hired assassins?" Clint asked, wondering how the lieutenant would feel when he saw that quote in Jonesy's story.

"Uh, sure, why not? They were tryin' to assassinate you, weren't they?"

"Probably."

"You mean you admit it?"

"I mean, it's likely if they were hired to shoot anyone who was out in front of the Waldorf this evening, it was me. Were there any other famous—or infamous—people there?"

"Not that I can see."

At that point Jones came back with a mug of beer and set it in front of the lieutenant.

"Thanks, Jonesy."

"Lieutenant," Jones asked, "what can you tell me about a man named Vernon Weeks?"

"What? Weeks? Where did you hear that name?"

"From Mr. Adams."

Egan glared at Clint, but spoke to Jones. "Get lost, Jonesy. Go write your story."

"But—but it's not complete."

"Get lost!"

"Okay, Lieutenant," Jones said, "I'll put that down as a 'no comment.' " Jones nodded to Clint and withdrew.

"What did you tell him?"

"That Vernon Weeks hired those men to kill me because he's a coward and afraid to face me himself."

Egan opened his mouth to speak, then stopped, sipped his beer and said, "That might work. You want him to come after you. Yeah, that just might work."

"Tell me something, Lieutenant," Clint said, "when I mentioned Vernon Weeks in the hospital, you knew who I was talking about, didn't you?"

"I might have had an inkling—"

"You know about Vernon and Tyler Weeks, don't you?"

"I may have heard some stories—"

"And now Vernon is after Annie Oakley for some sort of misguided revenge. You could have warned her, you know."

"So far," Egan said, "nobody's given me any evidence that Vernon Weeks is even in New York, Adams."

"You want evidence?" Clint asked. "I'll get it for you."

"Good. Just make sure Weeks is walking and talking when you bring him in."

"Uh-uh," Clint said, shaking his head. "No guarantees."

"That's okay," Egan said, grinning. "I didn't mean it, anyway. It's just something I'm required to say, as an officer of the law."

He finished his beer and stood up.

"I'm not takin' you in, Adams," he said. "I'll leave you free to work things out with Mr. Weeks—or whoever. But do me a favor, will you?"

"Anything for you, Lieutenant," Clint said. "You know that."

"Try to keep the number of dead innocent bystanders to a minimum."

FIFTY-FOUR

"This is your last chance," Vernon Weeks told the second man.

"Not my fault," the second man said. "I sent five guys after him. Jeez, five! He stood there and shot 'em all down."

"I know, I know," Weeks said, "I was there, lyin' on the ground, remember?"

"You should've shot him in the back while you were down there," the other man said.

Weeks gave the man a withering look. "If you had ever spent even a hour in the West, you wouldn't have said that."

"Fine, fine," the man said. "Code of the West and all that."

"That's right," Weeks said. "I've been east and west,

my friend. Sometimes I find the most civilized people in the West."

"Why didn't you stay there?"

"Because this is where Annie Oakley is," Weeks said. "Besides, if I was in the West, I wouldn't be payin' you all this money, would I?"

"That's a good point."

"You got any more men?"

"I know lots of men who would kill an old lady for five dollars," the man said.

"You got any good men?"

"Those are expensive."

"You mean the ones you used today weren't?"

"Uh, well, no."

"You got greedy, didn't you?" Weeks asked. "You kept most of the money for yourself."

The other man didn't answer.

"Okay, look," Weeks said, "tomorrow's the day, because I can't afford to fool around anymore. You get your men together and take care of Adams tomorrow. I'm going out to Staten Island to finish this, and I'm gonna do it right in front of Cody. This'll show him he's been payin' money to the wrong people."

"Can I ask you a question?"

"Go ahead."

"Did your brother really shoot himself just because he got beat by Annie Oakley?"

Weeks's eyes flared, and for a moment the other man thought he'd gone too far.

"He was humiliated by that little girl," Weeks said, finally, "and I'm gonna return the favor. That answer your question?"

"Yeah," the man said, "that answers it."

Weeks had two fingers of beer left at the bottom of his mug. He finished it now and slammed the glass down on the table.

"Meet me here tomorrow morning, seven A.M."

"Will it be open?"

"I'll be here," Weeks said. "Don't worry about whether it's open or not. Just be here."

"Okay."

Weeks stared down at the man for a moment.

"What?"

"Don't fail me tomorrow," Weeks said, "because if this doesn't go off without a hitch, the last thing I'll do is find you and kill you. Do you understand?"

"Perfectly."

With that Weeks walked out the front door to Houston Street, turned and walked to the Bowery.

When Clint went back out the front door of the Waldorf, everything had been cleaned up—bodies, glass, etc. The only thing still evident was the chunks of cement the bullets had chewed out of the front of the building. Also, there was no glass in the front door, but it had been cleaned from the ground.

A doorman came up to him and said, "Can I get you a cab, sir?"

"Is the other doorman a friend of yours?"

"Yes, sir," he said. "His name is Charles."

"How's he doing?"

"It's my understanding that he'll be fine, sir."

"What's your name?"

"Philip, sir."

Still parked in front of the hotel was the cab Clint had

taken to and from Brooklyn. With Willis dead, apparently there was no one to claim it.

"What's going to happen with that horse and carriage?" Clint asked the doorman.

"I'm not sure, sir."

"Did you know the driver? Willis?"

"Yes, sir," Philip said. "He picked up people from the hotel very often."

"Did he have any family?"

"I'm afraid I didn't know him that well," Philip said.

"Okay," Clint said. "Do you know a bar called O'Herlihy's?"

"Down by the Bowery, yes sir. It's a dive. Would you like a carriage to take you there?"

Briefly, Clint considered taking the dead man's carriage, but he hadn't been down to the Bowery very often and would probably end up lost.

"Yes, I would," Clint said. "Thank you. Have it waiting for me, will you? I have to get something from my room."

FIFTY-FIVE

The cab let Clint off right in front of O'Herlihy's.

"You don't want me to wait for you, do you?" the driver asked, hopefully.

"No," Clint said to the nervous man, "you can go."

"Thank you," the driver said. "If you're smart, sir, you won't spend very much time here."

"I'll keep that in mind. Thanks."

The driver then snapped the reins at his horse and got out of there, fast. Clint looked up and down the street, almost expecting another attack. So far he'd been shot at from hiding and been directly attacked in broad daylight. Who knew what was going to come next? Before leaving the Waldorf, he'd gone back to his room to collect his modified Colt. The Colt New Line was in the hands of the police, and he wasn't about to walk around unarmed.

The Colt was tucked into his belt, and he had donned a jacket he could close over it.

With no attack forthcoming, he turned and walked into O'Herlihy's Saloon.

Jack Po was sitting at a table in the back of the almost empty saloon. When he saw Clint, he pushed his chair back as if he was going to get up. Clint waved him down and went to the bar to get a beer.

"You don't want a clean glass, do ya?" the bartender asked.

"Reasonably clean, if it's not a problem."

"Ah, I was jus' kiddin'," the big man said. "Here ya go. Enjoy. Two bits."

Clint paid for the beer and carried it to Jack Po's table. He was careful not to inspect the glass too closely.

"Nice place," Clint said.

"It's out of the way," Po said. "I don't always want to be seen. Have you got my gun?"

"No," Clint said, "but I've got mine." He took it from his belt and placed it on the table. Po eyed it suspiciously.

"You can put it away," he said.

"I don't think so."

"Why not?"

"Because I've got some questions to ask you," Clint said, "and I think the presence of the gun might help you to tell the truth."

"About what?"

"About why you're such a bad shot," Clint said, "and such a small target."

"What are you talkin' about?"

"I'm talking about the fact that not one shot you fired came anywhere near any of those men," Clint said, "and not one shot they fired came close to you. Would you care to explain that to me?"

"I'm a notoriously bad shot," Po said. "Why do you think I have such an old gun?"

"And the hired gunmen?"

"Apparently they weren't any better than I was."

"They were good enough to hit me." Clint had changed from his bloody shirt, or he would have showed it to Po. "They killed your friend Willis, and hit the doorman."

"Okay, Willis wasn't my friend," Po said, "and I'm sorry about the doorman, but I didn't have anything to do with it, Adams."

"I'm supposed to believe that your talents simply don't extend to shooting?"

"I'm not a marksman or a showman," Po said. "I'm a detective. How well do you think Delvecchio shoots?"

"Very well," Clint said. "I've seen him."

"Okay," Po said, "bad example. What about Egan? He's a terrible shot."

"I don't care what kind of shot Egan is," Clint said. "We're talkin' about you."

"Hey," Po said, "you came to me for help. Don't forget, I was recommended by your friend Delvecchio."

"Don't remind me," Clint said. "And I'll tell you what you told me about Willis—Delvecchio and I aren't friends. We worked together once a few years ago."

"Well, you seem to value his service," Po said, "and his opinion. If you don't want my help, I'll just go back to Brooklyn. Nobody there wants to shoot at me."

Clint eyed Po speculatively, not sure what to think of the man. He certainly had been of no use during the firefight. If Clint needed somebody to watch his back, it wasn't Jack Po.

"Maybe that'd be best."

"What?"

Clint took the gun off the table, tucked it back into his belt and buttoned the jacket.

"Maybe you better go back to Brooklyn," he said. "I won't be needing you, after all."

Po stared at Clint for a few moments, then said, "All right, fine. Just pay me for my time."

Again, Clint stared at the man. The time he'd given hadn't been very valuable. His information, however, had been corroborated—sort of—by Lieutenant Egan, so at least he'd been telling the truth about that.

"What do I owe you?"

Po named a price, which sounded high, but Clint took out some money and paid him.

"So that's it?" Po asked.

"That's it."

"What about my gun?"

"Get it back from Lieutenant Egan." And this time he said what he was thinking. "Although I don't know why you'd need it. You can't hit anything with it."

"Everybody ain't The Gunsmith, you know," Po said, just before heading for the door.

"Oh, I know," Clint said. "Believe me, I know."

Before leaving, Clint went to the bar again.

" 'nother one?" the bartender asked.

"No, thanks. Do you know the man who just left here?"

"The one you was sittin' with? Sure, that's Jack Po."

"So he's been in here before?"

"Never used to come in," the man said, "but started just about a year ago."

"Do you know a man called Vernon Weeks?"

Now the bartender leaned his elbows on the bar.

"Friend, I know Po, and I know Weeks, and I don't want to get into trouble," he said. "If you want to know if I ever seen them in here together, I ain't gonna answer."

"That's okay," Clint said. "I think you already did."

FIFTY-SIX

Clint didn't like what he was thinking. If Po wasn't trustworthy, and he'd been recommended by Delvecchio, then what did that make Delvecchio? And if Delvecchio was not trustworthy, and Clint had put him right in the room with Annie and Frank Butler . . .

Clint waited in the lobby for Annie Oakley, Frank Butler and Delvecchio to return from Staten Island. When the three walked in, he stood up and approached them.

"Hello, Clint," Annie said.

"Can I talk to you?" he asked Delvecchio. "Hello, Annie . . . Frank . . ."

"What about?"

"It's private," Clint said. "Annie and Frank can go upstairs."

"We were going to go into the restaurant and eat," Butler said. "Is something wrong?"

"Just something Delvecchio and I have to iron out. It'll only take a few minutes. We can do it in the bar."

"Will you join us to eat?" Annie asked.

Clint hesitated, then said, "Probably."

Puzzled, Annie said, "All right, then, but—"

"Let's go, honey," Butler said, steering her away, which Clint appreciated.

"What's wrong?" Delvecchio asked, as they walked to the bar. "And what happened to the front of the hotel? Looks like there was a war out there."

"There was," Clint said.

They went into the bar, got a beer each and then sat at a table while Clint told the detective what had happened that morning.

"Jesus," Delvecchio said, "in broad daylight. Somebody is desperate to get you out of the way. Where's Jack now?"

"I fired him."

Delvecchio looked surprised. "What for?"

"I don't trust him."

"Why not?"

Clint explained Po's participation in the "attack" and then related the conversation they had in the Bowery bar. Delvecchio considered everything he'd heard before he replied.

"So now you're wondering about me."

"Wouldn't you be wondering?" Clint asked.

"Sure," Delvecchio said. "After all, I recommended him."

"Can you explain his behavior?"

Delvecchio hesitated, then said, "I thought he was better than that. I mean, I've seen him shoot. He's not that bad."

"So he lied."

"Apparently."

"How does that make you feel?"

"Angry," Delvecchio said, confused, frustrated. "It makes me look bad—and, if I'm reading your attitude right, suspicious."

"Look," Clint said, "I'm just asking for some . . . re-assurance, or an explanation . . ."

"Clint," Delvecchio said, "I know that Po often oper-ates outside the law. It's a line I don't cross, and he does. Maybe he's crossed it once too often. But let me say that again—I do not cross that line."

Now it was Clint's turn to mull over what the other man said. Finally, he nodded and said, "All right."

"I'm going to have a word with Jack, and I'm not ever going to recommend him for a job again."

"I hate to ruin a friendship, but . . ."

"We're not friends," Delvecchio said. "At best we were colleagues, men in the same business who sent work each other's way. If he's gone wrong . . ."

"I guess that remains to be seen."

"Yeah," Delvecchio said, sourly.

Both men used their beers to try and wash the sour taste out of their mouths.

"Do you want to join Annie and Frank for a late sup-per?" Clint asked him.

"It's my job, isn't it?" Delvecchio asked. "How about you?"

"Sure."

As they started to rise, Delvecchio said, "Wait. What did Po tell you about Vernon Weeks?"

"He told me about Vernon and his brother Tyler."

"Tyler Weeks!" Delvecchio said. "That's the name I knew. Killed himself, right?"

"Apparently, after Annie humiliated him in a couple of contests," Clint added.

"I remember now," Delvecchio said. "They thought they were the best marksmen in the world—and they hired out, right?"

"Right."

"So Vernon is looking for revenge."

"Right again."

"Okay, wait . . . something else you said . . . the bar you met Jack at?"

"O'Herlihy's."

"On Houston?"

"Right."

"That's a badman's bar," Delvecchio said. "Not a good place to be, or be seen. Did you talk to the bartender?"

Clint nodded. "Asked him if he knew the two men, Weeks and Po," Clint said. "He said yes, but also said that he wouldn't answer whether they'd ever been in there together."

"Which, in itself, is an answer."

"Right."

Delvecchio shook his head. "Po and Weeks," he said. "Looks like I sent you right to the man Weeks is working with. What a coincidence, huh?"

"I hate coincidences," Clint said, "but I suppose I'll have to accept this one."

Clint stood up, but Delvecchio remained seated.

"What's the matter?"

"How could I be so wrong about someone?"

"It happens, I guess," Clint said. "Sometimes people aren't who they seem."

"Or who they used to be," Delvecchio said.

"Come on," Clint said. "We'll go and discuss it with Annie and Frank. There's two people who are what they seem, and always will be."

Delvecchio stood up and said, "I hope you're right."

FIFTY-SEVEN

Over dinner Frank Butler and Annie listened intently to both Clint and Delvecchio, and by the time they reached dessert they were ready to give their own opinions.

Richard, the same waiter who served Clint his breakfast every morning, brought their desserts.

"It's not your fault you put your faith in the wrong man," Annie said, to Delvecchio.

"You're not at fault either, Clint," Butler said. "Neither of you had any way of knowing what this man had become."

"Should you tell Lieutenant Egan?" Annie asked.

"I think Egan is waiting for this to sort itself out," Clint said. "It's funny."

"What is?" Butler asked.

"Jack Po was telling me what a good policeman Egan was," Clint said.

"That should have been your first tip-off, then," Delvecchio commented. "Egan is a terrible policeman."

"That's what I thought."

"So we have no one to count on but you and Delvecchio?" Annie said.

"You don't have to say it like that," Delvecchio said.

"Oh no," she said, "I didn't mean—"

"I was kidding," Delvecchio said, raising his hand. "Of course you didn't mean anything."

"So what do we do now?" Butler asked.

"Tell me how things went with Cody," Clint said, "and we'll go from there . . ."

Cody, Annie and Butler had worked on some ideas for an act, but now that Annie and Butler had heard the story of the attack in front of the Waldorf they were having other ideas.

"You can't work the Waldorf into a Wild West Show," Delvecchio said.

"No," Butler said, "just some kind of shoot-out, with Annie and Clint the heroes."

"What about them shooting against each other?" the detective asked. "Isn't that what Cody had in mind?"

"It is," Butler said, "and we'll get to that, too. We just need something else to go with it."

"That's show business," Annie said, with a smile.

"I think," Clint said, thoughtfully, "it would be best if we all went out to Staten Island tomorrow, together."

After work, the waiter Richard left the Waldorf by a side entrance that left him in an alley.

"Hello?" he said.

It was dark and he couldn't see.

"H-hello? Are you there?"

Gradually, his eyesight adjusted to the darkness outside and he saw the man standing there, leaning against the wall of the next building.

"Oh, there you are," Richard said. "I didn't see you standing there when I came out."

"What have you got for me, Richard?" Vernon Weeks asked.

"You said a hundred dollars?"

"That's right, I did."

"Well . . . they said they're all going out to Staten Island tomorrow," the waiter said, "to see Colonel Cody."

"All of them?"

"That's what they said."

"That's good, Richard," Weeks said. "That's very good."

"Now I get the hundred dollars?"

"Now," Weeks said, slipping a knife from its sheath beneath his jacket and pushing away from the wall, "you get what's comin' to you, Richard."

FIFTY-EIGHT

Clint met Annie Oakley, Frank Butler and Delvecchio in the lobby the next morning. When they went outside, Clint noticed that the dead man's cab had not yet been removed by the police. Clint turned to the doorman, Philip.

"Philip, we're going to take that carriage."

"Sir," the doorman said, "it doesn't belong to the hotel. I suppose you can take it if you want."

Clint gave Philip some money.

"That's not necessary, sir."

"Take it anyway," Clint said. "Just in case the police come for that carriage today."

Philip smiled and said, "What carriage is that, sir?"

"Good man, Philip."

Clint turned to the others and said, "Come on, I got us a cab. I'll drive."

"Why do we need this particular cab?" Butler asked.

"So we don't have to trust some strange driver to actually take us where we want to go."

As they all climbed into the carriage, Butler asked, "Do you know how to get to the ferry?"

"I figure Del knows the way."

"Not me," Delvecchio said. "I never go to Staten Island."

"What about you, Frank? Annie?"

"Not me," Butler said.

"Me, neither," Annie said.

"Okay," Clint said, taking up the reins. "I paid attention the last time we went. We'll figure it out."

"Why not take them at the ferry?" Jack Po asked Vernon Weeks.

"Because," Weeks said, "I want it to happen out there, in front of Cody."

"What's Cody got to do with it?"

"Killing Annie Oakley," Weeks said, "in front of Buffalo Bill Cody, who she respects, will be the ultimate humiliation for her."

"Vernon," Po said, thinking he was talking to a crazy man, "she'll be dead. She won't even know she's been humiliated."

"I'll know, damn it!" Vernon Weeks said. "I'll know, and that's what matters."

"Okay, fine," Po said, "we'll do it out on Staten Island. Now all we've got to do is get out there before they do."

"We will, if your men get here," Weeks said.

"Here they come now," Po said. "A dozen of the best guns New York has to offer."

"Why does that not encourage me?" Weeks asked.

FIFTY-NINE

Clint managed to find his way to the Staten Island ferry. They parked the carriage off to the side, hoping it would still be there when they returned.

Annie had told Clint that Cody was going to have Styles waiting for them on the other end, and true to the frontiersman's word, there he was when they got off the ferry.

Cody himself greeted them expansively when they arrived at the site. Other than him, though, there didn't seem to be many of his crew or performers around.

"The place looks deserted," Clint said.

"It's an off day, really," Cody said. "I let most of my people go into the city and have some time off. I've just got a skeleton crew—oh, and the chief."

When they had all stepped down from the carriage,

Styles drove it away. Cody shook hands with Clint.

"Glad you came out," he said. "We have some rehears-
ing to do."

"And we have to talk over some new ideas," Butler
said.

"New ideas?" Cody asked. "Whose?"

"Ours," Annie said.

"All right, then," Cody said, "let's talk."

On a hill not far away Vernon Weeks and Jack Po were
using a spyglass to watch the proceedings.

"Place looks empty," Po said. "Must be an off day or
something."

"You think I don't know that?" Weeks said. "I know
Cody's schedule by heart. Nobody else is here but a few
workmen and that old chief."

Weeks looked down the hill behind them, where the
other twelve men waited with the fourteen horses they'd
been instructed to bring along with them.

"How are we going to do this?" Po asked.

"Slowly," Weeks said, "very slowly. Come on, you and
I are gonna ride in."

"Alone?" Po asked.

"No, not alone," Weeks said. "We'll be together."

"I meant—"

"I know what you meant, you fool!" Weeks snapped.
"Just do as I say and earn your money, okay?"

"Yeah, okay," Po said, with a shrug. "You're the boss."

"Try to keep that in mind, Po," Weeks said, as they
walked down the hill, "and things will turn out just fine."

Clint, Cody and the others didn't get very far with their
discussion of new acts before they heard the sound of
approaching horses.

"Now what's this?" Cody asked.

"I think this whole thing might be coming to a head," Delvecchio said. "One of those men is Jack Po."

"And the other one," Frank Butler said, "is Vernon Weeks."

Clint looked at Annie, Butler and Cody. He and Delvecchio were the only ones who were armed—but he couldn't believe that Weeks and Po were alone. He looked around and thought he saw the sun glinting off something on a nearby hill.

When the two men reached them, they remained on their horses. Both were wearing guns in holsters, and Po's was a gun significantly more useful than the one he'd previously had.

"Got yourself a new gun, eh, Jack?" Clint asked.

Po, remembering that Weeks wanted to do all the talking, did not respond.

In fact, Weeks reinforced that the moment he spoke.

"I'll do the talkin', Adams."

"You must be the famous Vernon Weeks."

"The coward, you mean," Weeks said. "Oh yeah, I read your little comments in the *Morning Telegraph* today. Did you think I'd be goaded that easily?"

"You're here, aren't you?"

"I'm here because it's time to put this to an end."

"And how would you like to do that, sir?" Cody asked.

"You're the famous Buffalo Bill, eh?"

"I am."

"Well, Colonel Cody," Weeks said, "I'd like to face this here little gal of yours man to, uh, woman, to show who's the best gunhand there is."

"I think that can be arranged," Cody said. "Annie, do

you object to meeting this man in a contest that will put this to rest?"

"Of course not, Colonel," Annie said, "but I don't think that's what the man has in mind."

"The little lady is exactly right," Weeks said. "I'm talkin' about a showdown, Dodge City style."

"Dodge City sty—You can't mean that you expect Annie Oakley to face you in a . . . a street gunfight."

"That's exactly what I mean, Colonel," Weeks said. "The ultimate winner-take-all contest, wouldn't you say?"

"You're crazy," Cody said. "This woman is a showman, not . . . not a common gunman. The answer to that, sir, is no."

"I'm kinda sorry you said that, Colonel," Weeks said. "You speakin' for everyone here?"

"He is," Clint said.

"Damn right!" Frank Butler said.

Weeks looked at Butler.

"How about you?" Weeks said. "If she's Little Sureshot, don't that make you Big Sureshot? You want to face me in your wife's place?"

"I'll face you—" Butler started angrily, but Clint cut him off.

"He won't," Clint said, "but I will. You want a real Western showdown, Weeks? I'm your man."

"The Gunsmith," Weeks said. "Well, well, now that would be somethin', wouldn't it? Me shootin' you down in front of all these people, fair and square?"

"Weeks," Clint said, "that would be a miracle."

Weeks's face and eyes went cold at the insult.

"You won't do it," Clint said. "If you have any confidence at all, you would have faced me a long time ago."

"I'm not after you," Weeks said. "I'm after the little

lady, and if she won't take the easy way out . . . well, we'll just have to do this the hard way."

"And what way is that?" Clint asked.

"This way," Weeks said, and waved his arm over his head.

The others looked around them, but it was Clint who looked right at the hill he'd seen the reflection from. Suddenly, a dozen men appeared on horseback, all armed, and just sat there.

"Jesus!" Delvecchio said.

SIXTY

"You've got ten minutes to send her out to meet me," Weeks said. "Nobody else needs to die."

"We don't need ten minutes," Clint said. "We've given you our answer."

"I'm still givin' you the ten minutes to think things over," Weeks said. He wheeled his horse around and rode off toward his men, with Jack Po right behind him.

"Ten minutes isn't much time to come up with a plan," Delvecchio said.

"What plan?" Clint answered. "We just need to come up with some guns before fourteen armed men come riding in here."

"Guns?" Cody said. "We've got guns. Follow me."

Cody took them into a tent which seemed to be bulging with supplies.

"Annie supplies her own guns, but we have some for the other performers who don't have their own."

He threw open a trunk which seemed to be stuffed with guns.

"Most of them fire blanks, but we should be able to find something in there that Frank and Annie can use. I notice, Clint, that you and Mr. Delvecchio have your own."

"An extra rifle or two wouldn't hurt," Clint said.

"I have my own guns in my tent," Cody said. "You folks go through these and I'll fetch mine."

"I'm going to go out and keep an eye on Weeks and his men," Clint said.

"I'll come with you," Delvecchio said.

They went outside and saw the fourteen men sitting abreast on the hill.

"This is crazy," Delvecchio said.

"I know," Clint said, "but it'll all be over soon."

"I can't believe Po is with them."

"Sorry about that, Del," Clint said.

"Just makes me feel stupid that I was such a poor judge of character," the detective said.

"Happens to everybody at one time or another," Clint said. "Don't let it get you down, or make you lose faith in your future judgment."

"That won't be easy."

Annie and Butler came up behind them, carrying rifles. They handed Clint and Delvecchio one each.

"There's no way to know how they work," Annie said, "but they should work."

Cody reappeared with his gunbelt strapped on, a pistol on each hip, and his Winchester in hand.

"Anybody else around here that can use a gun?" Clint asked.

"No," Cody said, "just some roustabouts. I told them to keep their heads down. It's not their fight."

"It's not yours, either," Annie said, "any of you."

Cody chuckled and said, "We're makin' it ours, darlin'."

"This is so crazy," Annie said. "This madman's brother kills himself and he blames me for it. Leave it to a man to commit suicide because a woman beat him in a shooting contest."

"Kinda makes me glad I went the way I did," Butler said, "marrying the gal who beat me."

Annie gave him an elbow. Clint could see how nervous the two were. This was quite different from shooting at targets.

"Annie, Frank, listen," Clint said. "You haven't been through this before. Don't fire until I say so, no matter how badly you feel you should. Find cover. We've got to wait until they get good and close, and then make every shot count."

"Don't fire until we see the whites of their eyes?" Annie asked.

Clint grinned at her and said, "Exactly."

"Don't worry about us, Clint," Butler said. "We'll pull our weight."

Clint wasn't worried about them; he was just worried about the weapons in their hands. He only hoped the bullets that came out of these guns would fly reasonably straight.

"Nobody shoot at the girl," Vernon Weeks warned all of the other men. "I'll kill any man who puts lead in her. Got me?"

"We got it," Po said.

"What about The Gunsmith?" a man asked.

"Everybody else is fair game," Weeks said. "Cody, Adams, everybody, but don't anybody shoot at that girl. Understand? She's all mine."

"We understand, Weeks," Jack Po said. "Just be ready with our money when this is all over."

"You'll get your money."

Vernon Weeks looked at his watch. Being a man of his word, he was going to give them the full ten minutes before he and his men rode in there and shot them all down. He didn't care how many of these men he lost while doing it. None of them mattered. The only thing that mattered was getting revenge for Tyler.

"And don't forget the plan," he said.

Behind him he heard a man say, "Wow, this is just like the Wild West."

He thought that idiot would probably be the first one to die.

Clint picked out Vernon Weeks, recognizing the man by his Western garb. The others all wore Eastern clothes, even though they were sitting horses with Western saddles. They wore a variety of hats—bowlers, caps—but Weeks was the only one wearing a Western hat.

If Clint could take Weeks right out of his saddle, maybe that would deter the others from continuing. After all, he was the man paying them.

Suddenly, the fourteen men on the hill urged their horses on and came riding down.

"Here they come!" Clint yelled.

SIXTY-ONE

Most of the fourteen men began firing even before they were within effective range.

"Clint?" Annie said, her voice quavering.

"Not yet," Cody said, sighting down the barrel of his own rifle. "Wait for Clint."

Clint looked over at the others. They had each pulled over a barrel or knocked over a bench or a bale of hay to use for cover. Delvecchio and Cody looked calm; Annie looked frazzled, and Frank Butler wiped the sweat from his eyes with his sleeve. Clint knew he could count on Cody, felt he could on Delvecchio, but if Annie and Butler faltered, they were going to be in trouble.

The men were still shooting, and now their lead was striking the ground or whizzing by. Still, Clint did not give the order to fire.

"Clint . . . ," Butler said.

And still they came.

"Clint . . . ," Delvecchio said.

"Closer . . . ," Clint said.

"By God, man," Buffalo Bill Cody said, "you are going to use that gun, aren't you?"

Just as Clint was about to give the order to fire, the charging men split into three factions. One split left, one right, and one kept coming down the middle.

"Damn it, fire!" Clint shouted. "They're going to try to flank us."

Clint found Weeks and fired. He missed. The goddamned rifle pulled to the left. By the time he had adjusted, the man was gone. He must have veered off. Clint fired again, and this time a man flew from his saddle.

"Mine fires high!" Annie said.

"Mine to the right," Butler said.

"Make the adjustment, people, and keep firing," Clint said. "Cody, watch the left. Del, the right."

Cody and Delvecchio moved to cover those flanks. Lead was suddenly striking all around them, coming very close.

The riders on the flanks fanned out again and Clint realized that Weeks had made a good plan. Had he kept his men together, Clint, Cody and Delvecchio could have done some damage, with or without the help of Annie Oakley and Frank Butler. Now the men were fanning out, surrounding them, and they were in real danger.

This was going to turn out to be close work, and he didn't know if Annie or Butler would be up to that.

"Cody?"

"Yo?"

"Give Frank one of your guns!" Clint said.

"Gonna get close, ain't it?" Cody shouted. He turned and tossed Butler a pistol. The man caught it neatly, which was a good sign.

Clint fired and another man flew from his saddle. He heard Delvecchio fire and saw another man fall. As the men got closer, all the shots began to blend together, and Clint could no longer tell who was firing when. A horse went down and the rider scrambled away on foot. Other riders dismounted as part of the plan, and now some of them were in the compound.

"This is your camp, Cody," Clint said.

"This way!"

They all turned and followed Cody, who gave orders as they went.

"Clint and Delvecchio, the big tent is that way," he shouted, pointing. "Frank, Annie, good cover that way, where the wagons are. Go! Go!"

Cody melted away and Clint lost sight of him. He turned at the sound of a horse and saw a man trying to ride him down. He drew his Colt and fired once, hitting the man in the face and knocking him to the ground. The riderless horse ran on.

"Nice shot," Delvecchio said.

"Let's split up," Clint said. "Hit and run. Understand?"

"Got it!"

Clint went right, Delvecchio left, and they were on their own.

Weeks knew his plan would work. His men were now inside Cody's compound, and Cody, Adams and the rest were on the run. Weeks dismounted and, gun in hand, went in search of Annie Oakley.

•   •   •

Annie and Butler ran together to the cover of Cody's show wagons. Butler grabbed Annie and pulled her behind one.

"You stay here!"

"But Frank—"

"Weeks is after you, Annie," Butler said. "Stay here, and shoot anybody that comes near you, as long as it's not me or one of ours."

"Like I have to be told that?" she asked. She grabbed his face, kissed him and said, "Don't get killed, Frank Butler!"

"Same here!"

He turned and ran, and Annie was on her own, clutching the Winchester that fired high—but how much good would it do with the action this close? she wondered. Still, she was better with a rifle than a handgun. She gripped the weapon with both hands and waited . . .

Clint made it to the big tent, and as he entered two men came in from the other side. They spotted one another at the same time and slapped leather. The two men never had a chance, for they had walked into The Gunsmith's fight. Clint fired twice, and both men were down. He ran to them to make sure they were dead, then picked up their pistols. He put his own in his holster and, with one of theirs in each hand, went out the other side of the tent.

If he could find Annie, he could give her one of these guns.

Clint counted five dead on the other side by his hand. One by Delvecchio, that he knew of. He had no idea where the shots fired by the others had gone, but he had to give Cody at least one kill, maybe two. After all, he was using his own guns. So figure half of their number were dead already, and now they were all on foot, trying to find or avoid each other in the maze of Cody's Wild West Show.

But he felt that sacrificing these men was probably part of Weeks's plan. He probably didn't even care if *he* died, as long as he got to Annie Oakley.

Clint wasn't about to let that happen.

Delvecchio slowed and began walking softly. He heard gunfire from other areas, but where he was right now was quiet. He seemed to be between tents, almost in an alley between them, and that was a bad place to be. He took out a knife and cut a slit in the tent to his right, then slipped through it. Once again he put the knife away.

This looked like some sort of storage tent, and then he realized it was the one Cody had gotten the guns from. He ran to the tent flap, looked out and then stepped outside. Immediately he came face to face with a man.

Jack Po.

They both had their hands down, their guns at their sides.

"Well," Po said. "Looks like I might owe you an apology, Del."

"Yeah? For what?"

"I made you look bad with that recommendation to Adams," Po said. "Didn't mean that."

"Don't mention it, Jack," Delvecchio said. "It won't happen again."

"Not gonna recommend me anymore?"

"No," Delvecchio said, "I'm gonna kill you."

Po grinned, then quickly tried to bring his gun up. Nei-

ther man had any speed, but Delvecchio beat him by a
split second and they both fired.

Delvecchio's shot went straight and true and drilled Po
through the heart. Po's shot went wide, but still struck
Delvecchio in the right shoulder, spinning him around and
putting him down on one knee. That's where he was when
a second man appeared. The detective tried to bring his
gun up, but his arm was dead weight. The man smiled an
ugly smile and raised his gun.

Frank Butler stepped out from behind a tent and shot
the man dead.

Annie decided she could not just sit there, hiding, and let
all the men do her fighting for her. It wasn't fair. As soon
as she stepped out from behind the wagon, she came face
to face with two men who had been creeping about. They
both had guns in their hands.

The three of them froze.

Then the men smiled.

"You're lucky we got orders not to shoot you, little
lady," one of them said.

"But you're comin' with us," the other said. "Vernon
Weeks is waiting for you."

"He wants you all to himself."

They started to advance on her. Could she shoot them
when they weren't trying to shoot her? If she didn't,
though, they'd have her and would take her to Weeks.

She hesitated . . .

"You can't shoot us," one of the men said, holstering
his gun.

"Come on," the other said. "Just give me the rifle."

Unbeknownst to them she still had her derringer in her

pocket, and maybe it wasn't such a bad idea to finally come face to face with Vernon Weeks.

One of the men grabbed the rifle and yanked it from her hand.

SIXTY-TWO

William F. Cody was in a bad spot.

He stood stock still as a man appeared on his right, and another on his left. Cody's gun—the one he hadn't given to Frank Butler—was still holstered, and the two men were holding theirs.

"Lookee here," one of them said. "A real live legend of the West."

"Buffalo Bill hisself," the other man said.

Cody turned his head all the way to his left to look at one, and all the way right to look at the other. Suddenly, his shoulders slumped and he looked old.

"You boys don't want to do this," he said. "I ain't worth it. I'm just an old showman."

"Famous Indian Scout, that's what you were," one man said.

"Scourge of the Comanche," the other said.

"Look at you now."

"Please . . . ," Cody said.

"Let's have a showdown," the man on his right said, and holstered his gun.

"Yeah," the man on the left said. He holstered his gun. "Let's do 'er."

Now that they'd leathered their guns, Cody stood up straight and tall. Both men noticed a sudden change in the man, who didn't seem so old after all.

"Whenever you're ready, gents," Cody said.

Both men, as if realizing they had made a terrible mistake, grabbed for their guns. Cody smoothly drew his gun and dropped to one knee. He fired once at the man on his right, and then at the man on his left. Had he been wearing both guns, he simply would have fired both simultaneously, killing both men. That would have been a better *looking* trick—but this one was *actually* better. Not only had he killed both men, but the shot fired by the man on his left had struck the other man as well, whizzing right over Cody's head.

Cody stood up, ejected the spent shells, shoved in two live ones and then said to the two men, "I ain't ever even met a Comanch'. I done most of my fightin' against the Sioux and Cheyenne."

He left them lying there and moved on, first claiming one of their guns. He felt much better with two pistols around his waist instead of one.

Vernon Weeks stopped in his tracks as, suddenly, the shooting stopped. Jesus, had Adams and Cody killed all his men already? Where was Annie Oakley hiding?

That was when two of his men appeared, holding the woman between them.

Butler helped Delvecchio over to the wagons, where he had left Annie. As they got there, Clint Adams suddenly appeared.

"How bad?" Clint asked Delvecchio.

"I'll live," the detective said.

"The shooting has stopped," Butler said.

"Where's Annie?" Clint asked.

"I left her right here and told her not to move," Butler said. "When I find her, I'm gonna let her have it."

"All right," Clint said, "stay here with Delvecchio, Frank."

"But I want to—"

"You want to keep him from bleeding to death, don't you?" Clint asked, cutting off his protest.

"Well, yes, but—"

"Stay here. I'll find Annie."

Clint didn't wait for any more protests.

"Well, well," Vernon Weeks said, "the great Annie Oakley. Bring her over here, boys, where I can see her."

The two men dragged Annie over to Weeks, who was standing in front of a tent that looked familiar to her.

"Here she is, Boss," one of the men said.

"We get a bonus for bringin' her to ya, right?" the other man said.

"You get a bonus for being the only two left alive, it sounds like," Weeks said. "Let's get this over with before the others find us, if any of them are alive. Give her a gun."

"What?"

"Give her one of your gunbelts. We're gonna have it out, here and now."

"But, Boss—"

"Now, I said!"

But before either man could react, Weeks saw Clint Adams appear across the way.

"Kill him!"

Both men turned and drew on Clint. He calmly drew his gun and fired one bullet into each of them. Annie, thinking Clint needed help, drew her derringer and shot one of the men in the back. She then turned to fire the other shot at Vernon Weeks, but he grabbed her by the wrist and squeezed until she released the gun, then pulled her in front of him and pressed his gun to her head.

Now it was him and The Gunsmith.

Clint, seeing that Weeks was using Annie as a shield, holstered his gun. Behind him Cody and Butler appeared, with Delvecchio supported between them.

"Annie!" Butler shouted.

"Stand still, Frank!" Clint ordered.

"Weeks, you son of a bitch—"

"Shut up, Frank," Clint heard Cody say.

"What's the plan here, Weeks?" Clint asked, spreading his hands out. "Your men are all dead, and now you're outnumbered. Give it up."

"Give it up?" Weeks asked, a crazed look in his eyes. Annie's eyes were pretty crazed, as well. "You see what I got here? This is what I came for. I put a bullet in her head and I'm finished."

"Finished for good," Clint said. "We'll cut you down if you do that."

"You think I care?" Weeks said. "Okay, so things didn't go quite the way I planned, but I got 'er now. I'm gonna kill her in front of all of you, and you can't do a thing about it."

Clint knew he had to take the shot. It was the only chance Annie had. He had to draw a fire. He tensed, and . . .

. . . from the tent behind Weeks and Annie, Sitting Bull stepped out. The old chief had a big buck knife in his hand. Quickly, he snaked his left hand around to grab Weeks by the chin. He lifted and with his right hand brought the blade across Weeks's throat, slitting it from ear to ear. Weeks's face went slack, and he released Annie, who scampered away just before a torrent of blood would have soaked her.

"No one kills the daughter of Sitting Bull," the chief said.

EPILOGUE

Clint awoke six weeks later with Mae Sinclair next to him. His four-week run as Cody's top act was over, and he was leaving New York today—and not a day too soon.

He and Annie had made a good team; there was no doubt. They had drawn crowd after crowd, and as far as who the better marksman was, they literally took turns beating each other. There was no clear-cut winner, but Annie had told him one day she knew he was the better shot—all things considered . . .

"Why do you say that?" he'd asked.

"Because you were going to take the shot that day," she said. "Before Sitting Bull stepped out of his tent. You were going to draw and fire and save my life."

"I might have missed," he said, "and hit you, instead."

She shook her head. "Never would have happened that

way," she said. "You would have taken the shot and made it, and you knew it. That's what makes you better, that confidence. I could never have taken that shot with confidence. Not with another life hanging in the balance."

"Hopefully," he'd told her, "you'll never have to . . ."

Clint stared at the light coming in the window, watched how it made Mae's skin almost glow. She'd been warming his bed two or three nights a week during the run, and while she was an energetic bedmate, he was ready to move on. He thought briefly about the people he'd interacted with while in New York. It was never dull . . .

Lieutenant Egan had been satisfied with the story they all told him about what happened out on Staten Island that day. He even came to see the show a few times. Cody made him pay full price . . .

Delvecchio had recovered from his shoulder wound and Cody had paid him a bonus, and given him a job overseeing security, which Delvecchio did with his arm in a sling . . .

Annie Oakley and Frank Butler signed to work for Cody again, and would accompany him to Europe once again for a triumphant tour. Clint was happy for both of them . . .

Mae rolled over and her big breasts came into view, flattened out a bit but luscious nevertheless. Clint had a train to catch that afternoon, and had said his goodbyes to everyone but Mae.

He slid his hand down between her legs, put his mouth on her breasts and woke her up to do just that.